"Who knew meeting?" asked

"You think someone inside the CNP betrayed us." Lieutenant Pureza didn't phrase it as a question.

"If the bomb had been a random thing, I wouldn't ask," Bolan replied. "But when they follow up with shooters, it's specific. No one tailed me from the airport, so there has to be a leak."

"You're right," Pureza said. "What's your solution, then?"

"A solo op," Bolan replied. "Or a duet, if you're still in."

"You think I'd leave you at this stage?" Pureza asked. "I must still live with myself—the one person I can absolutely trust. But you understand I represent the law?" she asked.

"You walk. We'll try to stay out of each other's way."

"And Macario wins."

"No, he's done, either way," Bolan said.

Pureza took another moment, making up her mind, then nodded. "Right," she said. "Where do we start?"

MACK BOLAN ®
The Executioner

The Executioner®
Don Pendleton's

POWDER BURN

A GOLD EAGLE BOOK FROM
WORLDWIDE®

TORONTO • NEW YORK • LONDON
AMSTERDAM • PARIS • SYDNEY • HAMBURG
STOCKHOLM • ATHENS • TOKYO • MILAN
MADRID • WARSAW • BUDAPEST • AUCKLAND

For Sergeant First Class Jared Christopher Monti
3rd Squadron, 71st Calvary
Gowardesh, Afghanistan
June 21, 2006

Recycling programs
for this product may
not exist in your area.

First edition February 2011

ISBN-13: 978-0-373-64387-5

Special thanks and acknowledgment to
Michael Newton for his contribution to this work.

POWDER BURN

Printed in U.S.A.

How does one kill fear, I wonder? How do you shoot a spectre through the heart, slash off its spectral head, take it by its spectral throat?

—Joseph Conrad
1847–1924
Lord Jim

I can't kill fear, but I can touch the men responsible for terrorizing innocents and pay them back in kind, before they die. For now, maybe that's good enough.

—Mack Bolan

THE
MACK BOLAN
LEGEND

Nothing less than a war could have fashioned the destiny of the man called Mack Bolan. Bolan earned the Executioner title in the jungle hell of Vietnam.

But this soldier also wore another name—Sergeant Mercy. He was so tagged because of the compassion he showed to wounded comrades-in-arms and Vietnamese civilians.

Mack Bolan's second tour of duty ended prematurely when he was given emergency leave to return home and bury his family, victims of the Mob. Then he declared a one-man war against the Mafia.

He confronted the Families head-on from coast to coast, and soon a hope of victory began to appear. But Bolan had broken society's every rule. That same society started gunning for this elusive warrior—to no avail.

So Bolan was offered amnesty to work within the system against terrorism. This time, as an employee of Uncle Sam, Bolan became Colonel John Phoenix. With a command center at Stony Man Farm in Virginia, he and his new allies—Able Team and Phoenix Force—waged relentless war on a new adversary: the KGB.

But when his one true love, April Rose, died at the hands of the Soviet terror machine, Bolan severed all ties with Establishment authority.

Now, after a lengthy lone-wolf struggle and much soul-searching, the Executioner has agreed to enter an "arm's-length" alliance with his government once more, reserving the right to pursue personal missions in his Everlasting War.

Prologue

Bogotá, Colombia

"How are we doing on time?" Drake Webb asked his companion.

"Fifteen minutes early, sir," Otto Glass said.

Webb wore a watch, of course—and a Rolex, at that—but demanding mundane information from lesser mortals was one of the perqs that came with a counselor's rank in the U.S. Senior Foreign Service. Otto Glass, as chief of station for the Drug Enforcement Administration in Colombia, understood the rules and followed them.

Their limousine rolled northward, passing the Plaza de Bolívar on Webb's left, with the stately Catedral Primada on his right. Ahead, he saw the looming Palace of Justice, surrounded by uniformed guards armed with automatic weapons.

Webb hated talking drugs with the Colombians, but it consumed most of his time. Cocaine and coffee were Colombia's main exports to the States—one of those having sparked a war that never seemed to end. For the ten thousandth time, Webb wished that he'd been posted somewhere nice and quiet, where the worst problem he had to deal with was a silly tourist's missing passport.

"Do you think they'll go for it?" he asked the DEA man seated next to him.

"Yes, sir. If foreign aid's contingent on cooperation, they don't have a lot of choice."

"Except the old standby," Webb answered. "They could tell us, 'Yanqui, go home.'"

"That's unlikely, sir."

"Right," Webb agreed, and thought, More's the pity.

Being shown the door would make one headache go away, but it would cause a slew of other problems, starting with the ignominious demise of Webb's career. He hadn't waded through red tape and diplomatic crap for the better part of thirty years to simply flush it all away.

He wouldn't be the Man Who Lost Colombia, by God.

And drugs *were* critical to U.S. foreign policy—had been for decades. Webb knew that, agreed with all the reasons that had been explained to him when he was rising through the ranks, watching the hypocrites in Washington get ripped at parties after blasting dealers and their customers in speeches redolent of hell-fire and brimstone. He fully understood political reality.

It didn't matter that the current President's drug czar had told America the "war on drugs" was over, that the government would focus more on education, rehabilitation and the other touchy-feely bits, rather than on SWAT teams and no-knock warrants. On the front lines, in the trenches where it mattered, Webb knew that the war on drugs was only getting worse.

And he was in the midst of it.

Ground Zero, if you please.

"Okay, sir," Glass was saying, as their limo pulled up to the curb, suddenly dwarfed by the Palace of Justice, surrounded by green uniforms. "Step lively till we're well inside, and everything should be okay."

Step lively, hell. Did Glass think either one of them could outrun bullets? Or the shrapnel from a car bomb, if it came to that?

Tight-lipped, Webb said, "I'll do my best, Otto."

"Yes, sir."

A second later the door opened. Webb's bodyguards spilled from the limo, mingled with the uniforms, then Glass was out and Webb was following. They ran a gauntlet of machine guns toward the granite steps.

Webb braced himself for impact, wondering if it was true that no one ever heard the shot that killed them. Almost hoping it was true, to spare himself the last indignity of panic in the face of death.

And then they were inside, doors closed behind them, slowing to a normal walk. The welcoming committee was approaching, smiling, hands outstretched in greeting.

More red tape, Webb thought. More bullshit.

Situation normal.

"ALL POINTS READY. MOVE on my command."

Manolo Vergara heard no tremor in his own voice as he spoke into the Bluetooth wireless microphone. Despite the rush of raw adrenaline, his hands were steady on the broom he pushed across a highly polished marble floor.

Vergara heard his soldiers answer briskly, one by one, their voices small and disembodied in his earpiece. All were ready, stationed in their proper places, waiting for his signal to begin.

The baggy coveralls draping Vergara's slender form were large enough to hide a multitude of sins. In this case, more specifically, the denim cloth concealed a micro-Uzi submachine gun dangling from a leather sling beneath his right arm, and belt around his waist, made heavy by grenades. Each of his five commandos, likewise, had arrived for work that morning dressed to kill.

And none had been detected. No one had sounded an alarm.

A quarter century had passed since the last attack on Bogotá's Toma del Palacio de Justicia, and that had been a full-scale frontal assault by thirty-five members of the Movimiento 19 de Abril—M-19. No one believed that such a thing could be repeated in this modern day and age.

They were correct, of course.

Outside, police and military guards ensured that no strike

force could storm the Palace of Justice. Anyone who tried it would be cut down in the street or on the steps, before they crossed the threshold.

But who really looked at janitors these days?

Who gave a second thought to peasants taking out the trash?

What thirty men could not accomplish by brute force, a bold half dozen might achieve by stealth. Vergara's handpicked team had infiltrated the building's custodial staff one by one, over the past eleven months, performing scut work and pretending they were grateful for the opportunity to serve.

Until this day.

The order had been given. They were privileged to strike against the enemy that morning, each emboldened by the knowledge that if he should fall, his loved ones would be handsomely rewarded. Set for life, in fact.

They each had El Padrino's word on that.

Vergara steered his broom in the direction of the conference rooms, where soon his enemies would be assembled. They were already in the building. He knew their habits, their compulsion to be punctual. He could almost *smell* them, drawing closer to their destiny.

Delivered by a peasant's hand.

Perhaps there was some justice, after all.

OTTO GLASS HADN'T FELT relaxed since he was transferred to Colombia as chief of station for the DEA. But for the moment, after the predictably tense limo ride and the virtual sprint from curbside to relative safety, his stomach was beginning to unclench.

Glass lived by one simple rule: *no one* was safe in Colombia, period. Sudden death could strike anyone, anywhere, at any time. And those least secure of the lot were Americans working on drug interdiction programs.

Meaning Glass and his agents, for starters.

He'd been on the job for seven months and had survived three attempts on his life, while another half dozen supposed murder plots were logged and filed from native informants. Glass wore Kevlar whenever he set foot outside his office or downtown apartment, and slept with armed guards at his door.

This day, inside the Palace of Justice with Counselor Webb and a retinue of smiling Colombian officials, Glass felt as safe as he had at any time since he'd stepped off his flight from New York, at El Dorado International Airport.

Everyone had settled into chairs around the highly polished conference table. A deputy vice-minister of the interior and justice sat at the table's head, flanked by deputy commanders of the Policía Nacional de Colombia and the Departamento Administrativo de Seguridad. A deputy assistant from La Fiscalía General de la Nación—the attorney general's office—was also present. All of them had aides with tape recorders, legal pads and pens laid out in front of them. All of them were deputies for higher-ups who couldn't be bothered to show, or who feared being forced to make a decision on the record before witnesses from rival departments.

"I welcome all of you to this historic meeting," the vice-minister of the interior and justice said, beaming down the table with artificially whitened teeth. "I know all present share my wish that—"

When the door clicked, somewhere to his left rear, Glass turned toward the sound. He saw a slender, squirrel-faced man decked out in coveralls, bracing a push broom with his left hand. Glass had time to wonder why the coveralls were open nearly to his crotch, before he saw the janitor's right hand and recognized what it was holding.

"Down!" Glass shouted, lunging at Counselor Webb and dragging the startled diplomat down with him, seeking any cover he could find, as two more doors swung open and all hell broke loose.

The close-range gunfire numbed his ears, as Glass half rolled, half dragged Webb under the broad conference table. Glass drew his pistol, clutching it white-knuckled, and discovered that he didn't have a shot.

The frag grenade came out of nowhere, bouncing on the table, spinning once on impact with the floor, then wobbling toward him like an odd, green-painted Easter egg.

And in the final seconds of his life, all Otto Glass could do was pray.

El Dorado International Airport, Bogotá

Mack Bolan traveled light. His carry-on contained some extra clothes, sparse toiletries, a guidebook to the city and surrounding countryside. Nothing that might alarm security and raise red flags at either end of his long flight from the United States, with a short stopover in Mexico City.

No weapons, for instance, although he'd be needing them soon.

Bolan was early, by design. His contacts were expecting him for early dinner, in the city's northern quarter known as Chapinero, but he needed solo time before they met, in order to prepare himself.

First up, the wheels. He had a Pontiac G6 reserved with Budget in the main airport terminal. The smiling girl behind the counter photocopied "Matthew Cooper's" California driver's license, swiped his credit card—all bills meticulously paid on time, in full—and gave Bolan his keys.

Ten minutes later, he was rolling eastward on Avenida El Dorado, keeping pace with high-speed traffic as he left the airport's small city behind him. Downtown Bogotá lay nine miles distant from the airport, and he could've covered it within five minutes flat, except for a preliminary stop.

He made that stop in Ciudad Kennedy, a district in southwest-
ern Bogotá named for the martyred American president. Bolan's
guidebook told him that the area was Bogotá's most populous
district, home to fourteen percent of the city's population, but
he was only interested in one inhabitant.

The man had a pawn shop two blocks north of Calle Primero
de Mayo. He introduced himself as José and accepted Bolan's
nom de guerre without question. José's shop was a place where
money talked, and the merchandise that Bolan sought wasn't
displayed for public scrutiny. A visit to the backroom set him
up and took a bite out of his war chest, but the case had been
donated by a kiddie pimp in Jacksonville before he shuffled off
the mortal coil, and there was always more where that came
from.

When Bolan left the shop, he carried two fat duffel bags that
might have clanked a bit, if anyone was listening. He also wore
a Glock 23 semiauto pistol in a fast-draw sling beneath his left
armpit, two extra 13-round magazines pouched on the right for
balance. A Benchmade Stryker automatic knife with four-inch
Tanto blade was clipped on to his belt, for easy access.

Bolan put the duffels in the Pontiac's trunk, locked them down
and he was good to go.

Traveling naked always made the Executioner uneasy. He
could kill a man two dozen ways barehanded, but most shooters
wouldn't close within arm's reach if they had a choice. And as
for tackling more than two or three at once, if they were armed,
forget about it.

He was covered for all foreseeable contingencies: two rifles,
one for distance and one for assault work; a submachine gun
with suppressor for close quarters battle where stealth was required; a combat shotgun, just because; assorted hand grenades,
spare ammo for the different weapons, with accessories including
jungle camouflage fatigues and hiking boots.

His destination was Chapinero. Bogotá's most affluent district,
and the capital's banking and financial center, ranged along Calle
72. Bolan wasn't on a banking mission at the moment, though.

No hefty deposits or gunpoint withdrawals. His target was the stylish Andino Mall on Carrera 11 in Bogotá's Zona Rosa.

The Pink Zone.

He supposed the district had been named for its high concentration of gay bars and other amenities serving the bulk of Bogotá's LGBT community. There was more to the Pink Zone than gay life, however, including some of Bogotá's most popular restaurants, nightclubs and stylish hotels.

Still homeless in the city, Bolan didn't plan on checking into the Victoria Regia, the Andino Royal or any of their posh competitors. His contacts would be waiting for him at a relatively small sidewalk café, where they could watch the street and get to know each other briefly, prior to moving on.

Bolan would recognize his contacts from the photos Hal Brognola had provided, with their dossiers. One agent from DEA and one from the Colombian National Police, teamed to collaborate with Bolan in an atmosphere where trust was hard to come by and the lifespan of an honest law enforcement officer was often short.

Together, Bolan hoped they could accomplish something.

But if necessary, he could soldier on alone.

It wouldn't be the first time—or, with any luck, the last.

Bolan spotted the Andino Mall and made a drive-by, picking out the open-air café, sighting his contacts at a table set back from the curb ten feet or so. Three chairs, and one still empty. Waiting.

The soldier drove around the block and found a parking garage, grabbed a ticket and parked three floors above street level, overlooking Carrera 11. He locked the Pontiac and pocketed his keys, then found the outer stairwell and descended toward the busy street.

"THIS MAN WE ARE SUPPOSED to meet. What was his name, again?"

Jack Styles resisted the impulse to smile. He knew damned well that his companion hadn't forgotten the name. Arcelia Pureza never forgot anything.

"Matt Cooper," Styles replied, adding, "That's all I've got, aside from my HQ's assurance that he's pro material, experienced and off-the-books."

"Clandestine operations," Pureza said with a pretty frown.

"What else? After the latest…incident," Styles said, resisting the temptation to say *massacre* or *slaughter,* "Washington isn't about to send another diplomat."

"You understand my delicate position in this matter," Pureza said, telling, not asking, him.

"I understand your people have signed off on it," Styles said. "Or so I was led to believe."

"In the spirit, of course, they agree," his companion replied. "But in practice—"

"It's practice that matters," Styles told her. "If spirit could win this thing, we'd have had it wrapped up years ago."

Pureza nodded, toying with her wineglass on the tabletop. "Of course, you're right. But you must understand the mind-set, Jack. After the killings, it became a matter of machismo, yes? A case of proving that the government cannot be frightened or intimidated."

"But?"

"But anger fades," she said. "And resolution, too, *verdad?*"

"Sadly, that's true," Styles granted. "Which is why we're moving fast, before the brass can get cold feet."

She nodded, sipped her wine, then said, "It goes beyond that, though. My people may regret what they have set in motion, if the resolution is not swift and sure. If there is…how do you say it? Collateral damage?"

"That's how we say it."

"In which case," Pureza warned him, "the powers that be may attempt to distance themselves from the choice they have made. They may assert deniability, and leave us grabbing the sack."

Styles *did* smile then. "Holding the bag," he said, gently correcting her. "And, sure, I've seen it done. The trick is to deliver, make it quick and clean—or quick, at least—and then get the hell out of Dodge."

"Your Wild West, *sí*," Pureza said. "Let us hope that your plan does not become our Alamo, eh?"

"I'll drink to that," Styles said, and drained his beer mug, flagging down the waiter for a refill. While he waited, Styles scanned the street, checked out the foot traffic, focused on men who fit the soldier profile.

Whatever in hell that might be.

Styles wished he had a photo of Matt Cooper, to confirm ID on sight, but the guy was too hush-hush for that, apparently. Or maybe someone in the States was worried about leaks, a very real concern with any operation undertaken in Colombia.

So Styles was flying blind, with Pureza riding his tailwind on faith.

He hoped they wouldn't crash and burn.

"What time is it?" Pureza asked. She wore a watch, of course, but obviously had a point to make.

"He's got five minutes," Styles replied, after a quick glance at his Timex.

"And then we leave?"

Styles felt his temper fraying. "If you're getting nervous, you can bail out anytime."

"And leave you here alone?"

"I'm touched by your concern," he said, letting the sarcasm leak through, "but I can handle it."

"Support from my superiors is still conditional—"

"On letting you participate," Styles interrupted her. "I got the memo. But who are we kidding?"

"I don't understand."

"Look, I know that your government cares about drugs. The folks on top are pissed about what's been happening because it makes Colombia look bad. But face it, half the people offering condolences today are on the cartel's payroll, and they'll still be picking up their cash next week, next month, next year."

"Unless we stop them," Pureza said, with a glint of anger in her striking azure eyes.

"This shit's been going on, with variations, since the 1970s," Styles said. "I was in third grade when the Dadeland massacre gave Florida a wakeup call in 1979. You weren't even born, for Christ's sake!"

"And your point is?" He thought she looked pretty, even in her anger, trying to pretend she didn't understand him.

"The names and faces change," Styles said. "Lehder, Ochoa, Escobar, Londoño, Renteria—and Macario. They come and go, but none of them could operate for two weeks if your leaders really wanted to put them away."

"And in your own country?" she challenged him.

"Corrupt as hell, no doubt about it," Styles admitted. "But we don't build special prisons so that drug lords can maintain their lifestyle in the joint, then give them weekend leave to the Bahamas. We don't have Mafia bosses running for Congress or blowing up airplanes with a hundred people on board to kill one snitch."

Pureza aimed a finger at his face. "Listen, Jack—"

But she was interrupted as a shadow fell across their table and a deep voice asked them, "Am I interrupting something?"

"IS THAT HIM?" JAIME Fajardo asked.

"It must be. He's sitting down," Germán Mutis replied.

"Let me see him again!"

Fajardo sounded excited, reaching for the compact binoculars Mutis was using to spy on the sidewalk café from two blocks away. Murder always excited Fajardo, but he liked the big, important killings best.

"He's an American, all right," Fajardo announced.

"I think so, too," Mutis agreed.

They'd been expecting an American, another of the endless meddling gringos, but with no description that would help them spot him. Still, it was enough that the stranger would come from nowhere and sit down with two known enemies, Fajardo thought, a gringo DEA man and the cocky bitch from CNP headquarters.

"Shall I give the word?" Fajardo asked.

"Not yet," Mutis said.

"But—"

"Not yet! Are you deaf?"

Fajardo slumped back into a sulk. Mutis held out an open hand, received the field glasses and raised them to his eyes once more.

There was no rush to give the word. Mutis observed the new arrival, watched him order from a smiling waitress who seemed taken with his looks. Mutis hired women when he wanted them, and didn't have to ask if they were put off by his many scars.

And yet what was he waiting for? The weapon was in place, with Carlos Mondragón on station, waiting for the order to trigger it by remote control. Mutis was using a mallet to smash a mosquito, but he was a soldier who followed orders. His *padrino* wanted a message sent back to El Norte, and Mutis was not in the business of second-guessing his masters.

So, why not proceed?

It wasn't squeamishness. Mutis had built and detonated bigger bombs, inflicting scores of casualties on demand. He cared no more for the men, women and children passing along Carrera 11 than he might for a nest of ants in his yard. They meant less than nothing to Mutis. He was indifferent to their suffering and death.

But the targets intrigued him.

Germán Mutis derived no quasi-erotic pleasure from his work, as did Jaime Fajardo. Beyond the satisfaction of a job well done, he felt nothing when one of his bombs shattered buildings and lives.

He was, however, fascinated by his targets. It soothed him, in some way Mutis could not define, to see them, watch them go about the final moments of their business, and persuade himself that they were worthy of his best efforts.

This day the weapon was a classic ammonium nitrate and fuel oil—ANFO—bomb. It lacked the sophistication of C-4 or Semtex, but it was cheap and easy to make. More to the point, it delivered predictable impact on target.

The bomb, though relatively small by ANFO standards at a mere two hundred pounds, would send the message that El Padrino desired. It was packed in the trunk of a Volvo sedan, surrounded by jars filled with nails and scrap iron. The Volvo itself would provide further shrapnel, along with the flames from its shattered fuel tank. Parked across the street from the Andino Mall, it was well within range of his prey and ready to go.

As soon as Mutis gave the word.

But there was no rush. The gringos and their bitch weren't going anywhere. Mutis wished he could eavesdrop on their conversation, listen to them scheming, making plans to topple El Padrino unaware that their lives had been measured out in minutes on a ticking clock.

This was the part that Mutis loved, if truth be told. The power to reach out and cancel lives in progress, possibly to change the course of history itself. How many of the strangers whom he killed today might have gone on to greatness or produced child prodigies, if given time? Was a doctor strolling down the pavement who could cure AIDS or cancer? A footballer who was loved by millions—or who might have been, next year?

At such a moment, Germán Mutis felt like God.

And he could well afford to savor it a moment longer.

"You're Cooper," the man from DEA said, as Bolan took his seat.

"I am," Bolan agreed. "Been waiting long?"

"You're right on time," the harried-looking agent said, reaching for Bolan's hand. "Jack Styles. And this is Lieutenant Arcelia Pureza, of the Colombian National Police."

"Narcotics Division," the woman added, as she touched Bolan's hand, there and gone.

"Okay, so everyone's on board with this?" Bolan asked.

"I think that it would help," Styles said, "if we could clarify exactly what 'this' is."

Before Bolan could answer that, a waitress appeared at his elbow. He paused, tossed a mental dart at the menu before him and ordered tamales to be on the safe side, with Club Colombia beer for a chaser.

When the waitress wandered out of earshot, Bolan asked, "Which part are you unclear about?"

Styles glanced at his native counterpart, frowning, then turned back to Bolan and said, "The whole thing, I suppose. Look, we took a bad hit at the Palace of Justice, no question about it. I lost my chief of station, not to mention Counselor Webb. The Colombians, Jesus…the whole second tier of their federal law enforcement network was gone in one swoop."

"And the shooters were political?"

"Supposedly," Styles said.

"All six were members of the AUC," Lieutenant Pureza advised him. "That is the Autodefensas Unidas de Colombia. The United Self-Defense Forces of Colombia. We have confirmed their records and affiliations."

"And the AUC's a right-wing group," Bolan said.

"As in ultranationalist, pushing neo-Nazi," Styles replied.

"And you suspect they're working for Naldo Macario's cartel?"

"It's more than mere suspicion," Pureza said. "We have documented cartel contact and collaboration with the AUC. Macario supports the group with cash and cocaine, which members of the AUC then sell abroad or trade for weapons."

"And in exchange for that?" Bolan asked.

Frowning, the young lieutenant answered, "Members of the AUC protect his coca crops and his refining plants, harass his competition and dispose of troublesome officials."

"So, you know all this, and no one's crushed the operation… why, again?"

"There are complexities," she said, and glanced away, avoiding Bolan's gaze.

"Well, there you go," Bolan said. "I'm the ax that cuts red tape."

"And what's involved in that, exactly?" Styles inquired.

The waitress brought his beer. Bolan sipped it, savored it, then set the frosty mug back on the tabletop.

"The law's not working for you," he replied. "It really hasn't worked for decades, right?" Pureza was about to protest, but he raised a hand to silence her. "I understand, it's relative. Reform follows a cycle, like the weather. People make adjustments and decide how much corruption they can tolerate. But this Macario has thrown the playbook out the window. He's like Escobar on crank, no better than a rabid animal. While your two agencies are following the rules, playing connect the dots and trying to indict him, he keeps running people through the meat grinder, making Colombia look like a cut-rate slaughterhouse."

"We've done our best," Pureza said.

"It isn't good enough," Bolan replied. "If he was only murdering Colombians, the folks in Washington could hem and haw, debate some kind of sanctions, stall it out and hope he dies from cancer or gets flattened by a bus. But now he's killing U.S. diplomats and federal agents, reaching out to pull the same crap in the States that he's been doing here. That's absolutely unacceptable."

"We're with you," Styles replied. "I'm simply asking what you plan to—"

Bolan never heard the rest of it. A shock wave struck them, billowing across the street as thunder roared and sheets of window glass came crashing down on every side. The air was full of shrapnel, flying furniture and bodies, as he struck the pavement, rolling, covering his head instinctively with upraised arms.

The aftermath of any great explosion was a ringing silence, like the void of outer space. It took a heartbeat, sometimes two or three, before sound filtered back to traumatized eardrums. During the same brief gap, nostrils picked out the intermingled smells of smoke, dust, blood and burning flesh.

Bolan knew he was hit. Something had stung his left biceps and scored his thigh on the same side, but neither wound was serious. He'd leak, but he would live.

Unless there was a follow-up.

Squirming around on pavement strewed with bits of scrap and shattered concrete, Bolan looked for his companions. Styles was laid out on his back, unmoving, with the bright head of a nail protruding from his forehead, just above a glazed left eye. There was no need to check his pulse to verify that he was gone.

Arcelia Pureza was alive and coughing, fingers probing at a

raw slice at her jawline. Bolan went to her on hands and knees, clutching her arm.

"Come on," he said. "We need to move."

"What? Move? Why move?"

The gunfire started then.

"That's why," he said, and yanked the woman to her feet.

2

The ANFO blast shattered windows for a block in each direction, paving Carrera 11 with a crystal layer of glass. Smoke roiled along the street and sidewalks, human figures lurching in and out of it like the undead in a horror film. Most of them looked like zombies, too, with vacant eyes in bloody faces, caked with dust and grime as if they'd just climbed out of graves.

"Goddamn it!" Germán Mutis snarled. "I can't see anything!"

"It's finally clearing," Jaime Fajardo said.

And he was right. After a lapse of seconds that seemed painfully protracted, Mutis saw the dust was settling, the smoke rising and drifting eastward on a breeze. He snatched the glasses back from Fajardo's hand and trained them on the spot where he'd last seen his three intended targets.

The chic sidewalk café was definitely out of business. Shrapnel had flayed the bright facade, turned plate glass windows into a million shattered pieces, and a compact car had vaulted from the curb, propelled by the concussive blast, to land inverted on the café's threshold. Bodies sprawled across the dining patio, twisted in boneless attitudes of death.

"No one could live through that," Fajardo advised.

But some of them *were* living. Mutis saw them rising from the dust and rubble, teetering on legs that had forgotten how to hold them upright, gaping with their dusty scarecrow faces at the carnage all around them.

Never mind the drones. Where were the three he'd meant to kill?

If they were down, his mission was successful.

If they lived....

He focused on a body that had worn a charcoal business suit before the blast. What still remained of it may well have been the DEA man's garb. One leg was bare now, flayed of cloth and quantities of flesh, but Mutis scanned along the torso, found the bloodied face with something odd protruding from the forehead.

So, the nails had worked.

One down. And if the gringo policeman had died at his table, the other two had to be nearby.

He sought the woman first. Her clothing, while conservative, had been more colorful than anything worn by her male companions. Was the color known as mauve? He wasn't sure, but knew that he would recognize it when he saw it.

If it wasn't blown completely off her body.

It pleased Mutis to think of her as both dead *and* embarrassed, though the concepts struck him as a contradiction. Rather, the CNP would be humiliated by the vision of its agent lying nude and bloody on the street.

"I want to see!" Fajardo said, almost whimpering.

"Shut up!" Mutis snapped. "Is that...? Mother Mary! She's alive! The bitch is— And the other gringo!"

Mutis swiveled in his seat, barely aware when Fajardo snatched the glasses from his hand. In the backseat, Jorge Serna and Edgar Abello sat with automatic weapons in their laps, regarding him impassively.

"Get after them," Mutis snapped. "They must not escape! Quickly!"

The shooters moved as if their lives depended on it, which was, in fact, the case. A simple, mundane order had been given—take three lives and snuff them out. So far, Mutis had accomplished only one-third of his mission.

El Padrino would not understand.

He would not be amused.

Within the cartel Mutis served, success was commonly rewarded and failure was invariably punished. He had witnessed El
Padrino's punishments on several occasions—had been drafted to
participate in one of them, a grisly business—and did not intend
to suffer such a fate.

Better to kill the bitch and gringo, or die in the attempt.

Mutis sat watching as his gunmen crossed Carrera 11, jogging
in and out of bomb haze toward the epicenter of the blast. He
took the glasses back from Fajardo, focused them again to suit
his eyes and found the blasted killing ground of the café.

Both of his targets had regained their feet. They had been
bloodied, seemed disoriented at the moment, but their wounds
were superficial. Neither one of them was bleeding out, goddamn
it.

Even though he was expecting it, Mutis still flinched when
Serna opened fire, followed a heartbeat later by the sound of
Abello's weapon. Neither found their mark the first time, and
their two targets started running.

"What are you waiting for?" he raged at Fajardo. "For the
love of Christ, get after them!"

BOLAN HADN'T SEEN THE shooters yet and didn't care to. If he
could avoid them for the moment, reach his car and get the hell
away from there before police arrived, he'd be satisfied.

Payback could wait.

And so he ran, pulling Arcelia Pureza behind him until she
could run on her own and jerked free of his grip.

"Where's Jack?" she asked him, as they reached an intersection, traffic stalled by the explosion, driver's gaping.

"Dead," Bolan replied. "Come on!"

She kept pace with him, had to have heard the automatic weapons fire behind them, but still asked, "Where are we going?"

"The garage up here," he said. "I have a car. Save your
breath!"

A bullet crackled past him, making Bolan duck and dodge. He

couldn't outrun bullets, but in the confusion of the aftershock, with all the dust and smoke, the shooters likely wouldn't do their best.

Halfway across the street, a taxi driver took his best shot, swerved around the van in front of him and tried to jump the intersection, going nowhere fast. A stutter burst from Bolan's rear stitched holes across the taxi's windshield, nailed the driver to his seat and froze his dead foot on the cab's accelerator. Bolan and Pureza cleared the lane before the taxi shot across and plowed into a storefront on the south side of the street.

"Ahead and on the left!" he told Pureza, in case she'd missed the thirty-foot bilingual sign that read *Estacionamiento*/Parking.

They reached the open doorway that served the garage's stairwell, and Bolan steered Pureza inside. "Third level," he told her. "Look for a gray Pontiac G6."

"You're not coming?" she asked him.

"I'll be right behind you."

As he spoke, Bolan drew his Glock and turned to face the intersection they'd just crossed. No other motorists had replicated the cabbie's mistake. From where the soldier stood, the cars within his line of sight looked empty, their occupants either lying low or already out and running away from the gunfire.

Bolan caught his first glimpse of the shooters, a mismatched pair, the tall one with lanky hair down to his shoulders, the short one crew-cut to the point where he looked like a skinhead. Both carried weapons that resembled AKS-74U assault rifles. They could be knockoffs, but it wouldn't matter if the men behind them found their mark.

Bolan squeezed off a shot at the tall guy, saw him jerk and stumble, then regain his balance for a loping run that took him out of sight behind a minivan. The short one, when he swung around that way, had already found cover of his own.

Too bad.

Bolan had missed his chance to end it here, but he still hoped escape was possible. It would be inconvenient—not to mention costly—if he had to leave the rented car with all his hardware in the trunk and start again from scratch.

Still better than a bullet in the head, but damned annoying anyway.

He took the concrete stairs three at a time, sprinting to catch up with Pureza and make the most of their dwindling lead.

ARCELIA PUREZA WAS FRIGHTENED. No point in denying it, as she was running away from a slaughterhouse scene with gunmen behind her, trying to finish her off. Styles was dead, she was injured, though not very badly, and she was stuck with a stranger who might or might not have a clue as to how to keep them alive.

She had not drawn her SIG Sauer SP 2022 pistol while running after Cooper on the street, but Pureza did so now, as she mounted the stairs to the parking garage's third level. Logic told her there were probably no gunmen waiting for her inside the garage, and yet…

Pureza reached a door marked with a two-foot number "3" in yellow paint and paused to peer through its small window of glass and wire mesh. The view was limited, but she saw no one lurking anywhere within her line of sight.

She entered the garage proper, holding her pistol down against her right thigh, index finger curled around its double-action trigger and ready to fire at the first hint of danger. Pureza had never shot another human being, but her recent brush with death convinced her that she would not hesitate.

She started scanning vehicles, looking for the Pontiac G6. He'd said that it was gray, but for the life of her, Pureza couldn't picture the car in her mind. So many modern sedans resembled one another, regardless of make and model. Cars used to be distinctive, almost works of art, but these days they came in cookie-cutter shapes, distinguished only by their small insignia.

Where was Cooper when she needed him?

As if on cue, the metal door banged open at her back. Pureza spun around, raising her SIG in a two-handed shooter's stance and framed the big American in her sights before she recognized him, saw his hands rise with a pistol in the right and let her own gun drop.

"Down there," he said, and pointed to his right along the line of cars nosed into numbered parking slots facing the street they'd left behind. "About halfway."

Bolan keyed the doors, making the taillights flash with a short beep-beep sound for people who couldn't find their car.

Pureza didn't stand on chivalry. She got in on the passenger's side, still holding her SIG at the ready, while Cooper slid into the driver's seat.

"I saw two shooters," he informed her, as he turned the key and revved the car's engine. "May have winged one, but I can't say for sure. If they're climbing the stairs, we may miss them."

"Unless there are more on the street," she replied.

"I wouldn't be surprised."

"Right, then."

Pureza found the proper button on the armrest of her door and lowered her window, while Cooper did the same on his side. Rental cars didn't have bulletproof glass, so the windows would be of no help in a fight. Also, raised windows would hamper defense and might spray blinding glass if they shattered.

Cooper backed out of his slot, shifted gears, and then they were rolling, following big yellow arrows spray-painted on pavement and wall signs that read Salida/Exit. Pureza knew they were starting on the third level, but it still seemed to take forever, circling around and around past cars that all looked the same.

Then she saw daylight, people flocking past the entryway to the parking garage, mostly hurrying toward the blast zone. Were they planning to help? Loot the dead? Simply gawk at crimson remains of catastrophe?

Cooper leaned on the Pontiac's horn, made no effort to brake as they sped toward the exit. She saw no cashier in the booth to their left, no one to raise the slender mechanical arm that was blocking their path. Beyond that fragile barrier, Pureza saw faces turned toward the sound of their horn and growling engine, people scattering.

And one who stood his ground, raising a gun.

"WHERE ARE THEY? CAN you see them?" Mutis barked into the mouthpiece of his hands-free two-way radio.

Static alone replied, at first, then one of his advance men— maybe it was Mondragón—answered, "They're inside the garage. One of them, the man, took a shot at Edgar."

"I'm all right," Abello said, interrupting. "The bastard just grazed my arm. I'm on the street exit."

"I'm going up to find them," Serna added, sounding short of breath. "We have them now."

"Make sure of it," Mutis commanded, then swiveled to face his driver. "Why in hell aren't we moving?"

"You see the street," Fajardo said. "All that glass, eh? We can't chase gringos on flat tires."

"Then back up and go around the block, for Christ's sake! Must I drive, as well as think?"

"No, sir!" Fajardo muttered something else as well, but Mutis couldn't hear it and the car was moving, so he didn't care. By then, he'd drawn a Walther MPK submachine gun from the gym bag at his feet, leaving its wire buttstock folded as he cocked the L-shaped bolt and set the selector switch for full-auto fire.

Fajardo boxed the block, first making an awkward and illegal U-turn in the middle of Carrera 11, then powered back to Calle 182, turned right and roared through the long block leading to Carrera 12. Another right turn there, and they were weaving in and out of traffic, letting pedestrians fend for themselves, in a mad rush northward to Avenida 82. There, he made a final right-hand turn and aimed the Mercedes back toward Carrera 11.

Time elapsed: five precious minutes.

"What is happening?" Mutis demanded, fairly shouting into the mouthpiece, although he knew it was unnecessary.

Hissing silence was the only answer for a moment, then Mondragón came back on the air, cursing bitterly. "Shit! They got out! Edgar's down, maybe dead. I can't tell."

"Which way are they going?" Mutis asked, teeth clenched in his rage.

"Northbound, toward—"

Mutis lost the rest of it, as Fajardo shouted, "There!" He saw a grayish car speed past on Carrera 11, barely glimpsed the gringo driver's profile in passing.

"Get after them!" he snapped at Fajardo. Then, into the mouthpiece, "You, too, Carlos! Run them down!"

"I'm on it!" Mondragón replied, with snarling engine sounds for background music.

Mondragón flashed past them in his blue Toyota Avalon, stolen for use as a spotter or crash car, as needed. He drove like a racer—and had been, on various tracks, before he recognized that El Padrino paid his drivers more than one could make on any local track.

Fajardo was talking to himself under his breath as he tromped down on the accelerator and sent the Benz squealing in pursuit. Mutis hoped that he wouldn't spoil the paint job, but if forced to make a choice, he would protect his own skin every time.

Missing the targets with a bomb, by chance, could be explained. Letting them get away when they were dazed and wounded was another matter, altogether. And if they had killed one of his men...

Mutis refused to think about the punishment that might await him if he took that news back to Naldo Macario. Better to shoot himself first and be done with it, skipping the pain.

But better, still, to finish the job he had started and step on his targets like insects, grinding them under his heel.

The thought made Mutis smile.

So far, so good.

Bolan had crashed through the garage retaining arm with no great difficulty, while Pureza took down the gunner who had challenged them with a decisive double tap. Falling, the guy had fired a burst that ricocheted from concrete overhead but missed the Pontiac completely, then they made the left-hand jog onto Carrera 11 and started the long northbound run.

It took only a moment for the first chase car to show up in the rearview mirror. Bolan knew it wasn't just another car headed in their direction, from the way it raced to overtake them, nearly sideswiping a pickup and a motorcycle in the driver's rush toward Andino Royal.

"We've got a tail," he told Pureza, then saw a larger black car closely following the blue Toyota. "Make that two."

"It's best if we do not involve the Bogotá police," Pureza said.

"Or any others," Bolan added. "Right, then. Are you up for fighting?"

"We're already fighting," she replied.

"Good point."

He held a straight course on Carrera 11 until they passed a large estate with wooded grounds on the right, then made a hard right-hand turn onto Calle 88 eastbound. More trees on both sides of the road, but Bolan knew that they were running out of residential neighborhood, with Avenida Alberto Lleras Camargo four blocks ahead. He'd have to make a move before that intersection, or risk carrying their firefight into rush hour traffic.

"On our right," he said. "Hang on."

Bolan swerved into a parking lot that served a cluster of high-rise apartment buildings, putting the Pontiac through a tight 180 that made its tires squeal and left Bolan facing back toward the street they'd just left.

The one-man chase car wasn't far behind, making the turn into the parking lot with room to spare. The driver had his window open, left arm angling some kind of stubby SMG toward the G6, where Bolan and his shotgun rider crouched behind their open doors with pistols leveled.

They squeezed off together, three rounds apiece, peppering the Toyota's windshield. Behind the glass, a screaming face flushed crimson and the blue car swerved away, leaping the curb of a divider, plowing over grass and slamming hard into a row of parked vehicles.

No one emerged from the wreckage, and Bolan dismissed it, turning back toward the parking lot's entrance. A black Mercedes-Benz appeared, nosing in a bit more cautiously than the Toyota, but determined to advance. Its passenger was firing by the time the Benz finished its turn, a compact submachine gun stuttering full-auto fire.

The natural reaction was to flinch from those incoming rounds, but the Executioner stood his ground, framing the shooter in his Glock's sights with a steady six-o'clock hold. Ten rounds remained in the pistol, and he triggered four in as many seconds, watching the 165 grain Speer Gold Dot JHP slugs strike home with 484 foot-pounds of destructive energy.

His first shot tore into the gunman's shoulder, while his second sent the SMG tumbling from spastic fingers. Number three drilled the guy's howling face, and the fourth shot was lost through the Benz's windshield.

Good enough.

In the meantime, Lieutenant Pureza was nailing the driver with one-two-three shots through the windshield, another swerve starting, this one to their left. The Benz passed Bolan's door with two feet to spare, losing momentum on the drive-by, but still traveling fast enough to buckle its grille when it struck one of the parking lot's tall lampposts.

"Are we done?" Pureza asked him, as the echoes faded.

"Done," Bolan said. "Let's get out of here."

3

Usaquén District, Bogotá

Jorge Serna was nervous. Not excited, as he'd always thought that he might be if he was called to meet with El Padrino. Not at all convinced that he would even manage to survive their meeting.

Survival, under certain circumstances, was a grave mistake.

He should have been impressed at passing by the lavish Country Club de Bogotá with its vast golf course, so close to the Mercado de las Pulgas flea market, but a world apart from bargain shoppers. Serna should have been dazzled by the sight of Unicentro, one of Colombia's largest shopping malls, or the elite shops at Santa Ana Centro Comercial, but all of it was lost on him.

His last day?

That still remained to be seen.

El Padrino's estate was surrounded by seven-foot walls topped by broken glass set in concrete. The only access, through an ornate wrought-iron gate, was guarded by armed men around the clock. Their number varied: never less than two, sometimes six or seven if the need arose.

On this day, he counted five men on the gate, armed with the same Tavor TAR-21 assault rifles carried by members of

Colombia's Urban Counter-Terrorism Special Forces Group. The guns resembled something from a science fiction film, but Serna knew they were deadly, with a cyclic rate of 750 to 900 rounds per minute on full-auto fire.

Only the best for El Padrino's personal guards.

As the limousine approached, one of the guards rolled back the gate by hand. Small talk within the family claimed that the gate had once been operated by remote control, with a motor and pulleys, until a power failure made El Padrino a captive within his own walls. Workmen had been routed from bed after midnight, in the midst of a fierce thunderstorm, to overhaul the system and return it to manual control.

Passing through that gate, Serna wondered if he would be breathing when he left the property. Or whether he would *ever* leave.

Another rumor claimed that El Padrino had a private cemetery on the grounds, or that he fed the bodies of the soldiers who displeased him into the red-hot maw of a specially designed incinerator, sending them off in a dark cloud of smoke.

Serna had smiled at those stories, with everyone else.

But he wasn't smiling at this moment.

He barely registered the vast house, wooded grounds or soldiers on patrol in pairs, some leading dogs. The limo whisked along a driveway, circling the mansion to deposit Serna and his escorts at a service entrance, at the rear. Another pair of soldiers met them there and nodded for them to go inside.

At the last moment, as they crossed the threshold, Serna felt a sudden urge to bolt, run for his life, but where could he go? Surrounded by walls and by men like himself, who would kill without a heartbeat's hesitation, what would be the point?

To make it quick, he thought, and shuddered.

"Are you cold, Jorge?" one of his escorts asked. The others laughed.

"I'm fine," he said.

"We'll see."

They ushered him into a large room—were there any *small* rooms in the house?—with bookshelves on the walls rising from floor to ceiling. At the center of the room stood El Padrino, paging through a massive tome atop a bookstand. It looked like maps or some kind of atlas.

"Jorge," Naldo Macario said, "thanks for coming."

As if I had a choice, Serna thought. But he answered, *"De nada, Padrino."*

"You've had a bad day," his master said. "It shows on your face. May I offer you something? Tequila? Cerveza?"

"No, thank you, sir."

"So, direct to business then." Macario approached him, smiling underneath a thick moustache, hair glistening with oil and combed back from his chiseled face. "You failed me, yes?"

Serna could see no point in lying. "That is true, Godfather."

"I send five men to perform a simple task, and four are dead. The job is still unfinished. Only you remain, Jorge."

"I'm very sorry, sir."

Apologies were clearly pointless, but what else could he say? He had failed *and* survived, the worst combination of all.

"I know you're sorry," Macario said. "I see it in your eyes. But failure must have consequences, yes?"

Serna's voice failed him, refused to pronounce his own death sentence, but he gave a jerky little nod.

"Of course you understand," Macario went on. "Under normal circumstances, I would have you taken to the basement, and perhaps even filmed your punishment as an example to my other soldiers."

Serna felt his knees go weak. It was a challenge to remain upright.

"But these," El Padrino said, "are not normal circumstances, eh? For all your failings, it appears that I still need your help."

"My help, sir?"

"You saw the American, yes? Before he killed the others and escaped, you saw his face?"

"I did, sir."

"And you would recognize him if you met again?"

"I would." He nodded to emphasize the point, seeing a small, faint gleam of hope.

"Then it appears that you must live...for the moment," Macario replied. "Correct your error, find this gringo for me, and you may yet be redeemed."

"Find him, sir?"

"Not by yourself, of course." His lord and master smiled at that, the notion's sheer absurdity. "With help. And when you find him, do what must be done."

"I will, sir. You can count on it."

"His life for yours, Jorge. Don't fail a second time."

THE SAFEHOUSE WAS AVERAGE size, painted beige, located on a cul-de-sac north of El Lago Park in Barrios Unidos. Bolan turned off Avenida de La Esmeralda and followed Pureza's directions from there. She unlocked the garage, stood back to let him park the Pontiac, then closed the door from the inside.

They had been lucky with the G6, in the circumstances. It had taken only two hits, one of them a graze along the left front fender that could pass for careless damage from a parking lot, the other low down on the driver's door. Nothing to raise eyebrows in Bogotá, where mayhem was a daily fact of life.

Pureza led the way inside, through a connecting door that kept the neighbors from observing anyone who came and went around the safehouse. They entered through a laundry room, into a combination kitchen–dining room that smelled of spices slowly going stale.

"You use this place for witnesses?" he asked Pureza.

"That, or for emergencies. I think this qualifies."

"No clearance needed in advance?"

"If you are asking who knows we are here, the answer would be no one."

"No drop-ins expected?"

"None."

"Okay. Who knew about our meeting?" Bolan asked.

"You think someone inside the CNP betrayed us." The lieutenant didn't phrase it as a question.

"If the bomb had been a random thing, I wouldn't ask," Bolan replied. "But when they follow up with shooters, it's specific. No one tailed me from the airport, so there has to be a leak."

"Why must it be on my side?"

"I'd be asking Styles the same thing," Bolan said, "if he was here. My only contact with the DEA is dead."

"So you're stuck on me."

"The phrase would be 'stuck *with* you,' and that isn't what I said. You've done a good job, so far. I'm impressed, okay? But someone had to tip the other side about our meet."

"You're right," Pureza said, relaxing from her previous defensive posture. "I was assigned by my commander, Captain Rodrigo Celedón. Above him, I can't say who might have known."

"You trust your captain?"

"With my life," she said.

"Be sure of that before you talk to him again. Because it *is* your life."

"The DEA may have a leak, as well."

"It happens," Bolan granted. "But they're getting whittled down in Bogotá these days, and I don't picture Styles setting himself up to be hit."

"What's your solution, then?"

"A solo op," Bolan replied. "Or a duet, if you're still in."

"You think I'd leave you at this stage?"

"It wouldn't be the dumbest thing you ever did," he told her frankly.

"I must still live with myself," Pureza said. "One person I can absolutely trust."

"And you're on board with what I have to do?"

"That part has been…shall I say *vague?* I was assigned to help with what is called a 'special case.' Beyond that, all I know is that the cartel wants you dead. And me, as well, apparently."

"That sums it up," Bolan said. "Naldo Macario wore out his welcome with the massacre at your Palace of Justice. It's crunch time. I'm the last resort."

Pureza held his gaze for a long moment before speaking. "So, we aren't building a case for trial," she said at last.

"The trial's been held. The verdict's in. Macario's outfit is marked."

"You understand I represent the law?"

"The system's broken down," Bolan replied. "We're trying an alternative."

"If I refuse?"

"You walk. We try to stay out of each other's way."

"And Macario wins."

"No, he's done, either way."

The lieutenant took another moment, making up her mind, then nodded. "Right," she said. "Where do we start?"

Department of Justice, Washington, D.C.

THE TELEPHONE CAUGHT Hal Brognola reaching for his hat. It was an hour and a half past quitting time, and he was taking more work home, as usual. He might have let the call go through to voice mail if it hadn't been his private line. Leaving his gray fedora on its wall hook, Brognola snagged the receiver midway through its third insistent ring.

"Hello?"

"Sorry to catch you headed out the door," the familiar voice said from somewhere warm and far away.

"So you're into remote viewing now?" Brognola inquired.

"Just safe bets," Bolan replied. "When was the last time you cleared the office on time?"

"Thirteenth of Never," Brognola acknowledged. "I forget the year. Aught-something. How's it going where you are?"

The private line was scrambled, but Brognola took no chances. Paranoia wasn't just a state of mind in Washington—it was a tried and true survival mechanism.

"Heating up," Bolan said in reply. "There was an unexpected welcoming committee and we lost our guy from pharmaceuticals."

Meaning Jack Styles from DEA. Brognola hadn't known him personally—the agency had something like fifty-five hundred sworn agents, more than twice that many employees in all—but he still felt the sharp pang of loss.

Once a cop, always a cop.

"So, you need a new contact?" he asked.

"Negative, at least for the time being," Bolan replied. "I've got some local help. We'll try to muddle through."

"If there's a problem with the local shop…"

Brognola paused and Bolan filled the gap. "We've talked about it. This one's good, so far. Not sure about the rest."

"Okay," he said reluctantly. "If you need any help, I should be able to provide it."

He slipped in the reference to Able Team, who'd gone to bat with the Executioner more than once, their link preceding Brognola's promotion at Justice and the creation of Stony Man Farm. Bolan and two of the Able Team warriors had traveled through hell together as outlaws, before they dropped off the grid to help Uncle Sam with his worst dirty jobs.

"I hope that won't be necessary," Bolan answered, "but I've got your number."

"Right," Brognola said. "But don't let the competition get yours."

"I'm still unlisted," Bolan said, and the big Fed could almost sense him smiling. "Later."

"Later," Brognola agreed, and cradled the receiver.

So the bad news from Colombia continued. The Justice man supposed he'd get a call from Stony Man Farm before too long, reporting details of the "unexpected welcome" Bolan had received in Bogotá. There'd be a call from DEA, as well, likely complaining that they never should have asked for Brognola's help in the first place.

As if it had been the agency's idea.

As far as Brognola knew, the DEA's top brass had no idea that Stony Man existed, much less what it actually did. The program was beyond top secret, authorized and created by a former President of the United States, maintained by that commander in chief's successors to deal with extraordinary situations.

If and when the program was exposed to public scrutiny, some heads were bound to roll, Brognola's and the current President's among them. Nothing in the U.S. Constitution provided for creation of a black-ops force like Stony Man, and while Brognola could defend it till doomsday on moral and practical grounds, the program didn't have a legal leg to stand on.

Virtually everything his warriors did was criminal, albeit for the classic greater good.

This time, Brognola grabbed his hat and put it on before another phone call could delay him. Stony Man, the DEA, or anybody else who sought a piece of him this night could reach him on his cell phone. He'd take the bad news as it came, meet the complaints head-on, without referring them upstairs. Unless it fell apart completely and his team could not complete a mission—something which, thank God, hadn't happened yet—he *took* calls from the Man upstairs, but didn't dial the hotline for a conversation on his own initiative.

It simply wasn't done.

Which put Brognola in mind of a saying he'd heard for the first time long years ago, as an agent in training at the FBI Academy.

Shit rolls downhill.

When Brognola's superiors, the President or the Attorney General, found something stinky in his in-box that demanded prompt covert attention, it came down to Brognola. Who, in turn, passed it down to Bolan, Able Team or Phoenix Force, depending on the circumstances. From there, with any luck, the worst load landed on the nation's enemies and buried them for good.

With any luck, Brognola thought. And hoped that Bolan's luck was holding in Colombia, where absolutely anyone could prove to be a lethal enemy.

LIEUTENANT ARCELIA PUREZA heard Cooper returning from the smaller bedroom of the safehouse, where he'd gone to make a call in private. She had resisted the burning temptation to eavesdrop, conscious that trust was their sole fragile bond.

But could she *really* trust this stranger?

The bombing and subsequent shoot-out in Chapinero had

shocked her. Despite the fact that violence was commonplace in Bogotá and nationwide, Pureza had been personally spared until that day. Not only was Jack Styles dead, and their best connection to the DEA was severed, but Pureza had also nearly been taken out—and she herself had killed for the first time.

It had been automatic in the given circumstances, a matter of instinct and reflex, where training and self-preservation combined. She was a bit surprised to feel no sense of guilt, but guessed that there might be delayed reactions, possibly reflected in her dreams.

Meanwhile, she had to think about Matt Cooper.

He was quick to point the finger of suspicion for the ambush at the CNP or DEA, but Pureza knew nothing of his own organization. Not even its name, for God's sake. How did she know that someone in the States—or the big American himself, for that matter—was not the traitor?

But she had to scratch Cooper off the list, since it was ridiculous to think he'd risk a bomb blast, then kill his own comrades, if he wanted Styles and Pureza dead. The wise thing would have been to dawdle, turn up late enough to let the bomb and gunmen do their work, then tell his headquarters that traffic had delayed him.

Better luck next time.

As for whoever might have sent him from the north to Colombia…

"All clear, then?" she inquired, as the man stepped into the living room once more.

"We're square with Washington," he said. "And you?"

"I still think that you're right. It's best if I don't call the CNP just yet."

And there, she'd done it. It was just the two of them, adrift in Bogotá and facing off against Macario's cartel, against the AUC, and anyone else El Padrino could think of to send against them.

Hundreds, at least. All happy to kill for a handful of pesos, or simply to curry Macario's favor. To earn a seat at his table.

Maybe thousands, then, instead of hundreds.

"Have you thought it through?" Bolan asked. "I mean, really?"

Pureza nodded. "Yes," she said. "I'm obviously marked. Macario never relents, once he's decided someone needs to die. My only hope, apparently, is pushing on with you."

"A stranger you don't know from Adam," he said, half-smiling. "And whom you have no good reason to trust."

"I didn't want to say it," she replied. "But, yes."

"It's only natural," the soldier replied. "If you weren't suspicious, I'd think you were crazy."

"Call me sane, then."

"Good. As for the trust, we've started building it. I can't believe you'd sit there waiting for the bomb, then drop those shooters, if you were on Macario's payroll."

Pureza felt her cheeks warm at the sound of her own thoughts, spoken by this man. "I can say the same for you," she said.

"Okay. We're straight on that, then. Next, you have to ask yourself what one man—or the two of us together—can possibly accomplish in the face of killer odds."

"You should become a mind reader," she said.

"I'm sticking to the obvious," Bolan said. "We've already cleared the first hurdle, trashed Macario's plan and sent four of his hardmen home in body bags. He'll be angry over that, and sometimes anger breeds mistakes."

"You're right about the anger," Pureza said. "His rage is almost legendary, and the punishments he metes out are…extreme. As for mistakes, he's made none yet that I'm aware of."

"Wrong. We've seen the first already," he said. "We're still alive."

"Is that a victory?"

"Damn right. Now all we have to do is *stay* alive and keep hitting Macario where it hurts most, until he runs out of steam."

"Perhaps you underestimate him," she suggested.

"I've been up against his kind before," Bolan replied. "They're tough, no doubt about it. But they're only human. Humans die."

"It's all-out war, then?"

"To the bitter end. If you want out, the time to bail is now."

"And spend the rest of my short life in hiding? No, thank you."

Her answer seemed to satisfy him. Bolan simply said, "Okay. We're good to go."

"One thing you must remember, Mr. Cooper."

"Make it 'Matt.'"

"All right. One thing you must remember, Matt."

"Which is?"

"We're only human, too."

4

"You trust him to deliver, Naldo, after he failed the first time?"

"It was a peculiar circumstance," Macario replied. "My guess would be that Germán failed to take enough men for the job. Jorge is normally dependable, and he's aware of what will happen if he fails a second time."

Esteban Quintaro didn't seem convinced, but he had not become the cartel's second in command by challenging Macario. Instead of arguing, he shrugged and said, "No doubt you're right."

"The DEA man was eliminated," Macario said. "That's something in our favor. It leaves—what, another six or seven in the city?"

"Eight," Quintaro said. "I have their names and photographs."

"I'm only interested in the ones who got away."

"We know the woman," Quintaro said. "Arcelia Maria Pureza, a lieutenant with the National Police assigned to the narcotics unit. She is thirty-one years old and lives at—"

"Have we tried to buy her, Esteban?"

"On two occasions. She declines our friendship."

"Foolish pride. Why is she still alive?"

"You never before gave the order to eliminate her, Naldo."

"You have her home address."

"I do."

"Put soldiers on it. If she turns up there, they should attempt to bring her in alive."

"Alive, Naldo?"

"For questioning. I wish to know the name and the affiliation of her gringo friend."

"With that in mind," Quintaro said, "I've checked at El Dorado and prepared a list of new arrivals from the States. There were fifteen gringos traveling alone, six more in pairs. Our friend at DAS is gathering a list of their hotels."

"Check all of them," Macario replied, knowing before he spoke that the instruction was unnecessary.

And he worried that it might be a wasted effort, too. The stranger, whomever he was, might well be traveling under an alias. There was a fifty-fifty chance that when they learned his name at last, it wouldn't help.

"While you do that, Esteban," he continued, "reach out to our friend in Washington."

"The congressman from—"

"Yes. It's doubtful he'll know anything about such matters, but there is a chance—a small one—that he can assist us. The American police kowtow to politicians."

"And if he can't help?" Quintaro asked.

"Thank him for trying. Send him a bonus."

Quintaro's face revealed his personal opinion of rewarding failure, but he wisely left the words unspoken. "As you wish, Naldo," he said.

"What's your opinion, then? About our man of mystery," Macario inquired.

The question seemed to take Quintaro by surprise. In truth, Macario seldom sought his lieutenant's opinion. He preferred to give orders and leave Quintaro to carry them out. On this occasion, though, he tried a different tack.

"He won't be DEA," Quintaro said.

"Why not?"

"If he'd been sent from Washington, officially, he would

have met them at the U.S. Embassy, not in the Pink Zone. He's avoiding contact with the diplomats."

"Which tells us...what?"

"He's unofficial, operating off the books. Perhaps the CIA?"

"They aren't involved in drug investigations," Macario said.

"As far as *we* know," Quintaro replied. "Under the so-called war on terror, who can say?"

The man had a point. Macario's attacks on various American officials, culminating with the massacre at the Palace of Justice, could be enough to put the CIA on his trail. Which would mean what, exactly?

In the old days, before Macario was born, the CIA had schemed to eliminate various targets. They'd failed repeatedly with Castro but had scored with Che Guevara in Bolivia, Allende in Chile, plus others in Africa and Asia. Such "executive actions" were forbidden these days, at least on paper, but Macario understood that reality often deviated from public policy.

"I want the gringo, Esteban," he said. "Make it your top priority."

"*Sí, Jefe.*"

"When you find the woman, he should be nearby. If not, she'll know how to reach him. See to it that she tells you."

"And if she resists, Naldo?"

"Subdue her. Use whatever force is necessary, but she *must* be fit for questioning."

"I'll speak to our doctor and have him standing by."

"Good thinking."

The doctor was a third-generation Nazi whose grandfather had avoided prosecution for war crimes by fleeing to South America, sampling the hospitality of Argentina's Perón and Paraguay's Stroessner before settling in Colombia under the Rojas regime. He had advised the army on interrogation methods, and supplied that same expertise to paying clients in the private sector.

Viva free enterprise!

"I won't detain you any longer from the hunt," Macario announced. "Keep me updated on your progress, eh?"

"Of course, Naldo."

If Quintaro resented the dismissive tone, he didn't let it show. Alone once more, Macario allowed his thoughts to focus on the stranger from America whose mission almost certainly involved Macario's destruction or imprisonment.

To El Padrino, they were much the same. He was determined that he would not live inside a cage. And any man who sought to kill him would be utterly destroyed.

With any luck, by Macario's own hand.

ASIDE FROM ITS CAPITAL District, surrounding Bogotá, Colombia was divided into thirty-two "departments," the equivalent of states or provinces. The Department of Tolima was southwest of Bogotá, once the domain of mountain-dwelling Pijao tribesmen, now an agricultural state known for the production of coffee and coca. Twin branches of the Andes Mountains, the rugged Cordillera Central and Cordillera Oriental, provided much of the raw material that was refined into cocaine by outlaw labs.

In short, prime hunting territory for the Executioner.

Bolan and Pureza drove the eighty miles from Bogotá to Ibagué, Tolima's capital city, over a two-lane mountain road resembling something from the wilds of Appalachia. Outside of Valle del Cauca in the far west, Colombia's highway infrastructure remains primitive, with patchwork repairs the general standard.

Bolan had no trouble with the Pontiac G6 in transit, holding his speed near the 48 mph limit established by law and keeping an eye peeled for highway police. Pureza, navigating, took the opportunity to brief him on the Macario cartel's operations in Tolima.

"Obviously, growing coca," she explained, "but the refinement is conducted here, as well. First they produce *basuco,* like brown putty, which some peasants smoke. From that, with more work, comes the cocaine hydrochloride you would recognize, in powder form. If the wholesale customers want crack, they finish the procedure on their own, after delivery."

"You have the labs spotted?" Bolan asked.

"Some, of course," Pureza said. "We never find them all."

"And those you do find?"

There was resignation in her shrug. "Some are destroyed. Others are warned to move. Some carry on as if the law did not exist. It all depends on the police commander. Regrettably, the standard of enforcement is inconsistent."

"Same thing in the States," Bolan admitted. "So what's on our hit list today?"

"East of Ibagué, in Piedras Province, there's a lab that I have been aware of for some time. Captain Celedón has been unable to locate it, even with the aid of satellite photographs. Perhaps we help him out today."

"Sounds like a plan," Bolan replied. "How is it for accessibility?"

"There is a road, of course, for transportation of the coca leaves and final product. We can use it to a point, but then must walk."

"I've got my gear," Bolan said. "Are you ready for a jungle hike?"

"I will be, when we've done some shopping in Ibagué."

"Right. You mentioned satellite shots of the lab?"

"That's correct."

"Do they offer any insight on security arrangements?" Bolan asked.

"The plant has guards, of course," Pureza replied. "In photos I have seen, there were at least a dozen men with rifles. Aside from them, *cocineros*—the cooks—supervise a peasant staff in preparation of the coca leaves. You know the five stages of refinement?"

"Not offhand," Bolan admitted.

"First comes La Salada, the salting," Pureza said. "Raw coca leaves are softened with calcium carbonate to release alkaloids. Next comes La Mojadura, the soaking in kerosene or gasoline to dissolve the alkaloids. In La Prensa, the pressing of leaves to recover the fuel. Next comes La Guaraperia, the separation, with the kerosene removed and ammonia added to the remaining product, which precipitates the alkaloids. Finally, La Secadaria—

the drying—produces cocaine. One kilo extracted from two or three hundred pounds of raw leaves."

"A lot of time and work," Bolan replied. "I aim to make sure it's a losing proposition for Macario."

"That's why he has the guards," Pureza reminded him.

"They go," Bolan said. "And the cooks. The rest can walk unless they want to fight about it. Then we torch the lab and hit the road."

"But first—"

"I know," he said, as they were entering the outskirts of Ibagué. "First, we shop."

"It won't take long, I promise you."

"No problem," Bolan said, checking the dashboard clock against the sun's position in the sky. "We want to hit the lab after it's dark."

"They work in shifts around the clock," Pureza told him.

Bolan nodded and replied, "That's what I'm counting on."

ESTEBAN QUINTARO ALWAYS enjoyed visiting Plaza de Bolívar— the heart of Colombia's capital city. The opulence reminded him of how far he had come from childhood in the slums of Medellín.

Standing beneath the plaza's statue of Simón Bolívar, Quintaro could see the Palace of Justice and National Capitol on the south side of the square; the French-style Liévano building, seat of Bogotá's mayor, to the west; the Vase House museum, where patriots demanded freedom from Spanish rule in July 1810, to the north; and to the east, the Primate Cathedral, headquarters of Bogotá's archbishopric.

He was surrounded by history and power, both impressed by its magnificence and pleased to know that many of the men and women laboring within those stately walls were owned by El Padrino, bought and paid for by the same blood money that Quintaro carried in his pocket.

And as Macario's anointed second in command, Quintaro owned them, too.

One of the serfs was approaching him on foot. Quintaro

checked his Dunhill Bobby Finder watch, confirming that the new arrival was on time and had not kept him waiting in the plaza, pleased to see the flicker of anxiety that crossed the other's face.

"I came as quickly as was possible, Mr. Quintaro," Cristiano Guzman said, sidestepping the amenities.

"You're punctual, as always," Quintaro said.

"Pleased as always that you've called on me," the politician lied.

"Which brings us to the reason for that call," Quintaro said.

Guzman was a deputy vice-minister with Colombia's Ministry of the Interior and Justice, operating four bureaucratic levels below the president. Most secrets held by the department lay within his reach.

"On this day, Mr. Guzman, one of your agents met with two Americans at the Andino Mall. There was…an incident."

"Of course!" Guzman bobbed his head, at the same time retreating a half step from Quintaro and crossing his arms. Defensive body language. "It is all the talk of Bogotá."

"One of the two Americans, a drug enforcement officer, was killed," Quintaro said.

"Yes, yes. The minister has been besieged by phone calls ever since," Guzman replied.

"My employer," Quintaro said, "is concerned about the repercussions of this incident, as you may well imagine. He is anxious to confirm that your officer and the second American suffered no lasting injury."

"Um, well…"

"He craves the opportunity to meet them both in person."

"Ah. In that regard—"

"I fear he will be satisfied with nothing less," Quintaro interrupted, stony-eyed.

"As I was about to say, sir, the officer of whom you speak is a lieutenant of the CNP."

"Her rank and name are known to us," Quintaro said.

"Her supervisor should have heard from her immediately following the incident of which you speak," Guzman pressed on, perspiring as he spoke, "but strangely, she has made no contact."

"You are sure of this?" Quintaro asked.

"Indeed, sir! The minister himself has ordered that she be located with all possible alacrity. A search is under way throughout Bogotá."

"And the American survivor?"

"Ah. See, that is problematical."

"Explain."

"I've spoken personally to the officer's immediate superior, Captain Rodrigo Celedón, a decorated veteran of twenty-seven years. He was aware of an intended meeting with the DEA man who was killed, but claims no knowledge of a third participant."

"You say he *claims* no knowledge. Was he lying to you?"

Guzman blinked at that. "Nothing suggested it," he said. "Unless, perhaps…thinking back…a certain nervousness about him. I assumed it was a personal reaction to the bombing and his agent's disappearance."

"But he may know more than he admitted?"

"Anything is possible, sir," Guzman reluctantly agreed.

"Your task, then, is to find out if this decorated captain lied to you, in violation of his duty."

"Ah. I'm not entirely sure—"

"Will you find out? Or should I ask him and report that you declined to help us in this matter?"

"Jesus! I said nothing of the kind, Mr. Quintaro. I am always happy to cooperate, of course!"

"Our employer will be pleased to hear it," Quintaro said. "When may we expect your full report?"

"Possibly tomorrow or the next day?"

"No."

"The captain may have left his office for the day, and—"

"In the midst of such a crisis he will surely be on call," Quintaro said.

"Of course, just as you say. I'll speak to him within the hour."

"And insist that he withhold no secrets, under pain of discipline."

"It shall be done."

"In that case, I should not detain you any longer."

Nodding, muttering farewells, the deputy vice-minister retreated, moving toward his office with all the energy of a man on his way to the gallows.

Quintaro smiled at the analogy. If Guzman failed him, he would make the bureaucrat wish that he *had* been hanged. And having done that for his personal amusement, he would find some other means to learn the truth.

PUREZA KEPT HER WORD; their shopping break was brief.

On a street three blocks from city hall, they found a store that catered to hikers and hunters intent on exploring Tolima's mountainous landscape. There, the CNP lieutenant purchased sturdy boots, a long-sleeved shirt and pants in universal camouflage with a cap and mini-ALICE pack to match, a web belt, a Ka-Bar knife with leather sheath, together with a duffel bag to carry all the gear. Bolan paid cash, after agreeing that Pureza could repay him later.

"Have you done a lot of woodland hiking?" he inquired, when they were on the road again and heading northward out of town.

"My parents were not blessed with sons," she said, smiling. "Until a certain age, I was what you would call a Tommy boy."

"Tomboy," he said, correcting her. "Camping and hunting, all of that?"

"Well, my father would not kill for sport. It was a trait that I admire. He was a great outdoorsman, even so, and in Colombia, outdoors means mostly mountains."

Bolan guessed he'd have no problem with Pureza keeping up. "Okay," he said. "So, when we're out on foot, what kind of hike's ahead of us?"

"From safe concealment of this car, perhaps two miles. Darkness will make the trail more difficult."

"I have a GPS," he told her. "If you've got coordinates…"

"I do. But set the system so it does not speak aloud."

He almost smiled at that, resisting an urge to explain that he'd done this before. Reminders never hurt, and there was nothing supercilious in her tone.

When they were half an hour out of town, Pureza pointed Bolan to a turnoff where the pavement stopped abruptly. He slowed to twenty miles per hour for the next ten minutes, then followed his navigator's directions to a side track screened by trees and shrubbery that would conceal the Pontiac from any but the most determined search.

"I need to change," Pureza said.

"Me, too. You go first."

Bolan waited in the car while she shed her street clothes and replaced them with the camouflage hiking gear. While she was lacing up her boots, he walked around and changed behind the car, leaving his civvies in the trunk.

"I only have my pistol and the knife," Pureza said, when he returned.

"I brought a little something extra," Bolan told her, lowering his duffel bags of hardware to the ground beside the Pontiac.

Taking the M-4 carbine for himself, he offered her the choice between a Spectre submachine gun or the combat shotgun. Pureza chose the shotgun, a Benelli M3T with folding stock and a switch that converted the weapon from pump-action to semiauto fire on demand. She looked it over, then proceeded to load it with double-00 buckshot, seven rounds in the tube and one more in the chamber with the safety on. She stuffed the cargo pockets of her camouflage suit with extra rounds from Bolan's stash.

"All ready, then," she said.

Bolan repacked his other gear, then stowed it in the car's backseat. "And this would be your last chance to stand down," he told her. "No recriminations or hard feelings, if you'd rather sit it out."

"You think I have a choice?" she asked him sharply. "After all that's happened and my failure to report? At this point, I'm probably suspected in Jack's murder."

"Tell them you were kidnapped," he suggested. "Who'd dispute it?"

"So, you are chivalrous, as well as brave," she said. "With thanks, I will decline and see this through."

"Your call," he said, and palmed the GPS device. "You want to give me those coordinates?"

Pureza quoted them from memory, impressing Bolan once again. Long years had passed since he'd surrendered any latent prejudice he might have felt against the concept of a female warrior fighting side by side with men. Too many women, in his personal experience, had proved themselves for any doubts to linger in his mind.

And how many were still alive?

A few.

"All right," he said at last. "On the approach, I'll take down any guards I can without alerting everybody in the camp. But once it breaks, you know the drill. Nobody with a weapon walks away."

"I understand."

"The good news is, it's not for sport."

"It might be, though," the woman told him. "Just this once."

5

Lab duty was the worst. Not difficult, per se, since all Tomás Caycedo had to do was hang around and supervise the workers, keep track of the guards. But it was *boring,* and the smell was inescapable.

Ammonia. Kerosene. Sulfuric acid. Fumes from any one of them alone could sear Caycedo's sinuses and turn his stomach, but all three of them together made him giddy, like a victim of a wartime gas attack.

He'd actually brought a gas mask to the lab one time, acquired from an army surplus store in Bogotá, but the cookers and their peasant help had laughed behind his back, so Caycedo made do with the same flimsy surgical masks worn by everyone else in the rank forest camp. Their fabric theoretically prevented anyone snorting coke or any other chemicals involuntarily, but they did nothing for the smell.

Prowling the outskirts of the camp, lighting a fat cigar to fight the stench, Caycedo wondered what the fumes were doing to his lungs, the other organs of his body. It was one thing to ingest cocaine voluntarily, for pleasure, but the other chemicals were poisonous, for Christ's sake!

What would he do if working at the lab should give him cancer? Could he go to El Padrino and complain? Granted, a bullet in the head was preferable to months or years of suffering, but—

"How can you smoke those lousy cigarettes?" a mocking voice asked behind him.

Turning on his heel, Caycedo found Rafael Silva smiling at him, his own mask lowered beneath his chin like some ineffective bib. The AK-47 slung over one shoulder made his torso tilt a little to the right.

"You'd rather smell that shit day and night?" Caycedo asked.

"It earns my people money," Silva answered. "All I smell is victory."

Another dreamer. Silva was a sergeant in the Autodefensas Unidas de Colombia, presumably committed in his heart and mind to crushing leftist agitation in Colombia, pushing the government toward a militant form of nationalism. In that pursuit, the group had executed hundreds—some said thousands—of suspected criminals, radicals and critics of the AUC, actions that had earned the AUC condemnation as a terrorist group from the U.S. Department of State.

Meanwhile, the paramilitary patriots also served El Padrino, reinforcing his ranks as required, for a price. They guarded rural labs, escorted cocaine shipments and furnished troops for special projects such as the recent raid on the Palace of Justice.

"You heard about the incident in Bogotá?" Caycedo asked.

"The bomb?" Silva dismissed it with a shrug. "There's always something blowing up."

"I'm told this one could mean something to us. To everyone."

"Like what?" Silva asked.

Now it was Caycedo's turn to shrug. "I don't get details, only orders to be ready."

"So? We're always ready. Do you want to come with me? Inspect the troops?"

Caycedo thought about it, pictured trailing Silva all around the camp's perimeter to see a lot of cocky youngsters standing guard, and shook his head.

"Maybe another time."

"All right then." Silva turned away, smiling again. "Enjoy your cigarette, but don't set the camp on fire."

BOLAN SMELLED THE LAB when they were still a hundred yards downrange. The sharp tang of its chemicals was foreign to the woods that sheltered him, all cloaked in darkness. He paused and felt Pureza moving up beside him in the night.

She stood on tiptoe, leaning close to whisper in his ear, "How far?"

His answer would have been inaudible without near contact. "Say a hundred yards. We'll have to watch for guards as we move forward."

Bolan saw her nod in lieu of further spoken words.

They had proceeded slowly from the car, as nightfall overtook them in the forest. Bolan used his GPS to chart their course when daylight failed, and they were finally within reach of their target, closing for the kill.

He watched for booby traps, despite a hunch that none would be deployed for fear of picking off lab personnel who answered calls of nature in the woods. Likewise, high-tech security devices would require a generator, and its sound would have alerted him already. Battery-powered lamps would serve the cooks and guards, eliminating open flames and at the same time limiting their field of vision after sundown.

Good for the Executioner. Bad for those he'd come to find.

The first guard they encountered was a solitary lookout short on discipline. He couldn't do without a smoke while standing watch, which offered both visual and olfactory pointers to his location. Bolan left Pureza to cover his approach, then drew the Stryker automatic knife from his belt and opened it against his palm to muffle the distinctive click.

Maybe the guard was young and inexperienced. Maybe he thought the lab was safe from interference and it didn't matter how he passed the time. As grim death approached him from his blind side, he was humming salsa music, sifting restlessly from foot to foot in imitation of a dance.

Bolan waited until the guard lowered his cigarette, then clamped a hand over his mouth, trapping the smoke inside. A leftward twist bared throat and jawline for the thrust of tempered steel, slicing the jugular and the carotid artery, withdrawing for a second strike into the windpipe.

It was over in a moment, as the sentry slumped in Bolan's grasp. The Executioner lowered his burden to the forest floor, wiped off his blood-slick blade before he closed it and retreated toward Pureza's position.

She was ready with the shotgun leveled as he reached her, lowering its muzzle only when she recognized him. At his nod, the lieutenant followed Bolan on a path that would avoid the fallen sentry's corpse while making progress toward the forest laboratory.

Eighty yards and closing.

With an average dozen guards on-site, Bolan presumed that six to eight would be on watch at any given time. Pureza had pegged the lab's size as a rough quarter acre, including all structures, which meant a perimeter somewhere between 420 feet and 550 feet, depending on the layout. Figure one man every thirty yards or so, scattered through the woods in no regular pattern, and what were the odds of meeting another?

The answer—one hundred percent.

The second lookout was a wanderer, either assigned to keep moving or else unconcerned with the rules. Bolan saw him approaching, knew there was no way to avoid him, and went for his Glock with the sound suppressor fixed to its muzzle.

One shot was enough to dispose of the guard, but the dying man triggered a burst as he fell, churning leaves at his feet, shearing through his right foot. Already dead and gone, the sentry didn't feel a thing, but still he did his job.

"Come on!" Bolan snapped, as he broke into a run, racing to reach the camp as every man inside it sprang to full alert.

Rafael Silva was halfway through his circuit of the lab's perimeter when the short burst of autofire froze him in place, stopping dead in midstride. He mouthed a curse, turned toward the sound and broke into a run.

A clumsy accident, most likely. Someone walking with his finger on a weapon's trigger, contrary to standard discipline. It happened rarely, but in any situation where he had to deal with human beings, a mistake was possible.

Worse still would be a soldier who'd imagined that he saw a snake, maybe some other creeping thing, and lost his nerve. Silva had drilled his men incessantly, conditioned them to keep their nerves in check, but once again the human factor might betray him.

Silva was contemplating appropriate punishment when a second burst of fire erupted from a different quarter, closer to the lab. A shotgun blast immediately followed, startling Silva since no one in camp had a shotgun.

Intruders?

It hardly seemed possible, but—

The next blast, even louder, had to be a hand grenade. Silva unslung his rifle, flicked off its safety and revved up his jog to a sprint. There was no longer room for doubt.

The compound was under attack. But by whom?

Never mind.

Silva's duty was simple—protect the cocaine lab, its workers and product. If he failed in that his life was forfeit.

He reached the compound's clearing as another blast went off, this one demolishing a shed where chemicals were stored. A ball of flame shot skyward, rolling toward the treetops, searing imprints on his retinas. Silva blinked rapidly to clear his vision while he scanned the camp, disgusted by the sight of soldiers scrambling every which way, as if they had never spent a moment learning military discipline.

Silva raged at them, cursed them, grabbed one who was passing him and slapped the soldier's face. It sobered him and brought the young man's eyes back into focus, obviously fearing Silva more than any unseen enemy.

It was a start.

"Who is firing?" he demanded.

"I don't know, Sargento!"

"Come with me, then—no more running like a chicken with its head cut off, eh?"

"Okay!"

He steered the frightened soldier toward the prefab building that doubled as the camp's command post and communications center. With its shortwave radio Silva could reach the outside world and summon reinforcements. He had people in Ibagué who could reach the camp within—

The CP blew up in his face, the shock wave driving Silva backward off his feet. The tumble saved him, as a sheet of razor-edged aluminum came hurtling from the wreckage, caught his young companion underneath the chin and clipped his head as neatly as a guillotine.

Blood geysered from the stump and spattered Silva's face, filling his eyes. Before he had a chance to clear them, something hard and sharp ripped through his shoulder, rending flesh and bone.

All discipline forgotten, Silva screamed.

WHEN THE SECOND SENTRY went down firing, Pureza felt her stomach clench into a knot of fear. There had been no time for fright during her first gun battle with Cooper, as they were pursued from the Andino Mall, but through the hours that preceded their latest flirtation with death she'd had ample time to think.

Pureza was afraid, would have gladly bolted back in the direction of their hidden car, although she doubted she could find it in the dark. But when the big American rushed the compound she followed closely behind him.

She'd chosen this course and would see it through to the end.

As they entered the camp Cooper lobbed a grenade, ducking low in avoidance of shrapnel before it exploded. Pureza followed his example, scanning left and right for enemies, and saw one of Macario's gunmen running toward them.

She shouldered the Benelli shotgun, set for semiauto fire, and slammed a clump of double-00 lead through his guts, each pellet a .33-caliber bullet. Nine shots for one squeeze of the trigger, and then she moved on, trailing Cooper and watching his back.

The lieutenant was alert and ready when he pitched another frag grenade, this one delivered through an open window of a prefab hut with a radio antenna rising from its roof. Later, she guessed that the grenade had detonated fuel of some of the cocaine lab's chemicals, based on the fireball that erupted when the building came apart.

Pureza saw a human form lurch out of that inferno, wings of fire flapping as if in a vain bid for flight. The human torch was screaming and flailing his gun, and Pureza was about to silence him with her Benelli when a bullet out of nowhere found the burning man and put him down.

She was up and moving once again, somewhat amazed that she hadn't been shot already, since her enemies had begun firing on every side. Unfortunately for themselves, they couldn't seem to find a target, wasting ammunition on the trees, night shadows and one another.

Some were not disoriented, though. She saw Cooper drop two men as they were firing at him, bullets coming close enough that she imagined he had to feel their passing as a whisper on his skin.

And then it was Pureza's turn, as someone bellowed at her from her right-hand side and fired a pistol shot in her direction. Turning as she dropped into a crouch, Pureza could have sworn she heard the slug zip past one ear. She barely saw the gunman, didn't take aim and had no need to as the shotgun boomed, sending another spray of lead downrange.

Her target did a clumsy backward somersault and landed in a heap, unmoving but for twitches at his various extremities. Instead of watching while the life ran out of him, Pureza bolted for the nearest cover, yet another prefab structure at the north end of the compound.

Praying as she ran that Cooper wouldn't blow *it* next, and send her vaulting off into the void of death.

TOMÁS CAYCEDO HUDDLED in the shadow of an open shed where kerosene was stored in five-gallon cans prior to use in processing cocaine. He knew it was a stupid place to hide, but having found it in the midst of the chaotic battle, he was afraid to move.

No, not *afraid*.

That word was death if used in El Padrino's presence. Better to say that he was being cautious, waiting for a chance to face the enemy, rally his men and lead them on to victory.

But still, he did not move.

Caycedo clutched his pistol, a Mark XIX Desert Eagle chambered in .50-caliber Action Express, but there'd been no opportunity for him to fire it yet. In fact, aside from shooting on a range with earmuffs on, he'd never fired the massive weapon, which he'd purchased on a giddy whim for two thousand U.S. dollars.

Would the hand cannon prove its worth?

Not if he stayed beside the shed, waiting for it to blow and drench him in a bath of flaming kerosene.

Caycedo braced himself to run, then saw a target jogging toward him through the firelit chaos of the camp. It was a man he didn't recognize, dressed as a soldier, hung with bandoliers and weapons, carrying some version of the M16 assault rifle.

Take him now! Caycedo thought, raising his five-pound weapon with both hands and sighting hastily before he squeezed the double-action trigger. The Desert Eagle's recoil jolted him from wrist to shoulder, its report slamming his eardrums even with the other gunfire going on around him.

And he missed.

Was it excitement? Nerves? He'd obviously jerked the trigger, spoiled the shot, and squeezing off two more in rapid-fire did nothing to correct the situation. Both shots were wasted, though they might fly on to strike some unsuspecting forest dweller, but Caycedo reckoned that he'd never know.

The soldier whom he'd failed to kill was down and rolling, swinging his rifle toward Caycedo even as he dodged the wasted bullets. Bolting from his shadow-shelter, Caycedo ran for it, but a 3-round burst of 5.56 mm bullets caught him with a leg raised for his second stride.

The impact slammed Caycedo hard into the open shed, rebounding from the containers of kerosene. A second burst punctured some of the cans, which spouted amber fuel over Caycedo's face and chest. It burned his eyes and made him sputter as he wriggled painfully away, to keep from drowning in a flood of kerosene.

And then Caycedo saw the spark, a bullet glancing off one of the cans, perhaps. A scream was rising in his throat as heat and light enveloped him, his whole world going up in flames.

BOLAN SCANNED THE COMPOUND as the last of its unarmed employees slipped into the forest, vanishing from sight. Around him, bodies lay in twisted attitudes of death, unmoving, though the firelight made their forms cast eerie moving shadows.

On the far side of the camp, Pureza moved among the bodies, checking them for signs of life. Grim-faced, she held the shotgun ready, muzzle sweeping back and forth. Approaching Bolan, she seemed satisfied that no one from the lab's security contingent would be bouncing back to threaten them.

"We're finished here, I think," she said.

"As soon as we've disposed of all the product," Bolan answered.

It required a bit more time, locating cans of kerosene that hadn't been shot up or set ablaze, and spreading flames throughout the compound, leaving only one route of withdrawal to the west. Firelight illuminated the surrounding trees, while heat waves made them shimmer, almost as if they were dancing in a ring around a funeral pyre.

At last Pureza told him, "There's no more to burn except the dead."

But some of them were burning, adding their aroma to the stench of smoke and chemicals that made the compound's atmosphere unsavory. Retreating with Pureza to the tree line, Bolan turned his back on havoc, palmed his GPS device and started on the hike back to their ride.

Pureza was silent for the first half mile, then touched his elbow, speaking softly. "Is your life always like this?"

"Not always," Bolan answered. "But you've seen the worst of it."

That wasn't true, of course.

She hadn't seen the friends who'd fallen during the Executioner's long war against predators in human form. Pureza had experienced a taste of it during the afternoon, when Styles was killed, but Bolan guessed she'd never found a loved one savaged, mutilated, pleading for a mercy shot with frantic eyes.

He hoped she never would.

"So we have more of this to come," she said.

"Unless Macario and all his men line up in court to cop a plea," Bolan replied.

She had to smile at that. "They won't, you know."

"I wasn't counting on it."

"But you'll punish them for murdering Americans."

"Americans, Colombians, whoever," Bolan said. "For killing men, women and children. For the arrogant belief that they can get away with anything. The bottom line—because they're just too dangerous to live."

"And what of us? After tonight, are we still fit to judge?"

"I'm not their judge or jury," Bolan answered. "They've condemned themselves. I'm just their executioner."

6

Jorge Serna was nervous, with good reason. Visiting the home of a CNP lieutenant was dangerous enough, but if he failed to find her or at least locate some evidence of where she'd gone, he would be facing El Padrino's wrath with no excuses left to save him.

Bearing that in mind, he offered up a prayer to long-forgotten gods, wishing that he had time to make a proper sacrifice instead of floating empty promises.

La Castaña was one of some three dozen neighborhoods found in San Cristóbal, Bogotá's fourth district, located in the capital's southeastern quarter. San Cristóbal was named for Saint Christopher, revered in various traditions as the patron saint of travelers, bachelors, martyrs and victims of toothache.

Good for me, Serna thought, since he was unmarried and was traveling, after a fashion. Not to mention that he would be cruelly martyred if his mission proved a failure. All he needed was a toothache to hedge his bets across the holy board.

The target, Lieutenant Arcelia Pureza, occupied a small apartment in a building located on Calle 21 Sur. Serna had no realistic hope that she would be home, but even on the off chance he would have to check. And once inside, there was a search to be conducted, seeking…what?

El Padrino wanted to find the lieutenant, of course. But even more, he wanted to identify the tall American who had survived the ambush in La Zona Rosa. He was the true prize of Serna's quest.

The woman, if she was not wise enough to flee Colombia entirely, could be hunted down and killed at leisure. But the tough American was another story altogether.

El Padrino wanted him alive, if possible, for questioning and a protracted punishment. The very thought made Serna queasy, since he realized that he would take the gringo's place if he could not produce a victim on demand.

Luck had preserved him in the fight at the Andino Mall—who would have guessed that luck was bad?

Esteban Quintaro had assigned three men to join in Serna's hunt. Hector Vallejo drove their car, a stolen Audi A4 sedan, while Serna occupied the shotgun seat. Behind him, Fernando Marquez and Manuel Reyes sat with leather bags of weapons at their feet. They were prepared to kill, but only as a last resort.

"It's here," Vallejo said, pointing. "Brown building, on the corner."

Serna quickly analyzed the layout. Corner lots meant more exposure, but escape was often simpler. The sun had set long ago and it was dark, which reduced the visibility of witnesses, thus helping Serna's team.

Not *my* team, really, Serna thought. All three of his companions understood his situation, knew that he might be living on borrowed time, and none wished to share his fate if the quest proved fruitless. On the plus side, that should make them eager to succeed at any cost. The minus side—none of the three would hesitate to blame him if they failed.

They might even decide to kill him, thus ensuring that he could not contradict whatever story they concocted for Quintaro.

Over my dead body, Serna thought, and chuckled at the grisly truth of it.

"What's funny?" Vallejo asked.

"Nothing. Just find someplace to park."

"Sí, sí."

One trip around the block to check it out, then Vallejo parked the Audi two doors south of the lieutenant's small apartment building.

"Get ready," Serna ordered, clinging to the slim illusion of command.

Their weapons were a literal mixed bag. Serna's, a BSM/9 M1 submachine gun manufactured in Brazil, was a 9 mm Uzi knock-off using the original weapon's staggered box magazines, firing at a cyclic rate of 600 rounds per minute. Vallejo also carried a Brazilian SMG, the .45-caliber CAV M9M1. The backseat gunners preserved that trend toward diversity, Marquez packing a Chilean SAF machine pistol, while Reyes had chosen a Guatemalan SM-9, copied after the American MAC-10.

In addition to the automatic weapons, each man had at least one pistol tucked into his belt or snugged into a shoulder holster. All they needed were targets.

When all the SMGs were cocked and hidden under jackets, Serna muttered, "Let's go!"

In darkness, the four soldiers left their vehicle and started for the silent house.

"I NEED A SHOWER AND a change of clothes," Pureza said, wrinkling her nose as they drove toward Bogotá.

"We'll need to find another safehouse, then," Bolan replied. "You can't go home."

"I've thought of that. There is another place where we can stop. But clothes...that means more shopping, I'm afraid."

"As long as you don't mind me picking up the tab," Bolan said. "Credit cards leave too much evidence of where you've been."

"I'll gladly spend your money in a good cause."

"Not *my* money," Bolan said. "It was...donated to the cause."

"Should I inquire as to the source?" Pureza asked.

"Some guys who didn't need it anymore."

"You lead an interesting life."

"That's one way of looking at it," Bolan said.

"Will you rob Macario, as well, to fund another fight?"

"Given the chance," Bolan admitted. "Either way, I plan to hit him in the pocketbook."

"You've started that already," she observed.

"*We* have," he said, correcting her.

"It's strange, you know?"

"What's that?" Bolan inquired.

"Working for something all your life, then throwing it away like that." She snapped her fingers. "In a moment, everything you know is gone."

"That's overstating it, I hope."

"Is it? This morning I was a lieutenant in the CNP, expecting a promotion in the coming year. I had my share of commendations. Now, what am I? Nothing but a fugitive from the police and criminals alike."

"The last I heard, you have approval for this gig from your superiors," Bolan said. "So did Styles."

"I'm sure they never thought that Jack would wind up dead, or that I'd be in hiding like a criminal."

"You want to call your boss? Check in?"

Pureza thought about it for a moment, then shook her head. "No. Jack was right."

"About what?" Bolan asked.

"Whatever my superiors agreed to at the start, they'll have the cold feet now. If any document approved the plan, they will be hidden or destroyed. If I go in, I'll be sacrificed. A rogue agent— or worse, a *woman* agent whose emotions drove her mad."

"There's still the kidnap story, if you want to try it," Bolan said.

"In which case I become a bumbling fool, instead of a crazed vigilante," she answered.

"It looks like you're stuck, then."

"We're both stuck, I think," Pureza said.

"So we may as well take our best shot."

"And suppose we succeed? If the miracle happens, you're free to go home. In El Norte they'll call you a hero, perhaps. I stay here, with no job and no prospects, at best a pariah. At worst, as a prisoner."

"I may know someone who can help you out with that," Bolan replied.

"Oh, yes? You want to help me?"

"There's much more to be done before that discussion can take place," he said. "But if you need help when we're finished here, I'll do my best."

She eyed him skeptically, with just the hint of a smile. "And what would this help cost, exactly?"

Bolan laughed aloud at that, surprising her. "You think I'm going through all this so I can jump your bones?" he asked. "Get over yourself."

Pureza blinked at him, then joined in Bolan's laughter. "I apologize," she said at last, "for thinking you had any interest in my *bones*. In our society, the price of progress for a woman may be different than for a man."

"I know the score on that," Bolan admitted. "But it's not my style. No insult to your bones intended. As bones go, they're pretty nice."

"You see!" She grinned. "I knew it!"

"Busted," Bolan said. "But for the moment, I'm more interested in herpetology."

"Reptiles?" she asked him, frowning.

"Right. I came to cut the head off of a snake."

Usaquén District, Bogotá

"HOW MANY DEAD?" NALDO Macario inquired. His voice was calm, despite the storm of rage that roiled inside him, sparking an impulsive need to smash, destroy and kill.

"We don't know yet," Quintaro said. "The AUC had thirteen men on-site, besides our peasants for the scut work, and Tomás."

"He called you?"

"No. One of Garzón's men."

"That prick."

Captain Orlando Garzón of the CNP was a prick, and then some. He welcomed the fat envelopes filled with cash as if they were his due, and appeared to believe that he was untouchable. Macario looked forward to deflating that particular fantasy.

But first…

"We need more details, Esteban. First thing, locate survivors. Peasants, AUC, I don't care who they are. Obtain descriptions of the raiders. Find out whether one of them was an American."

"You think he's in Tolima now, Naldo?"

"If I knew where he was, I'd have my hands around his neck. That's what we must discover, Esteban. You understand?"

"Of course, Naldo. The men are searching everywhere."

"They must search *harder,* then. Call anyone and everyone who owes us *anything,* from Bogotá to Washington. I want this man's name. I want to know who sent him here, and why. I want to know where we can find him, and I want it this minute! If our men fail in that, let none of them return alive!"

Quintaro nodded, retreating toward the exit with eyes lowered. He was wise enough to know when any verbal answer was the wrong one and might bring the wrath of El Padrino down upon his head.

Alone once more, Macario crossed his office to the wet bar ranged along the southern wall. He opened a bottle of *aguardiente*—literally "burning water," distilled from various fruits or grains—and poured himself a double shot. The clear liquor scorched his throat and lit a fire inside his stomach, barely mellowing before he downed a second glass.

The goddamned Yanquis were insane if they believed that he could be intimidated by attacks on his home turf. Macario was a fourth-generation *proscrito,* an outlaw, immune to threats of punishment. He had been raised to scorn the law, live by his wits, shun mercy as a weakness of cowards. Only cowards backed down from a fight.

Unless, of course, they were setting a trap for their enemies.

Courage did not require foolhardy risks. More than once, Macario had lulled his adversaries by pretending to surrender, letting them believe that they had won the battle, then struck back at them with righteous fury when their guard was down.

But how could he bait a trap for a nameless, faceless enemy? Without communication, or at least some notion of the bastard's intentions, what could he do?

The raid in Tolima might be coincidental, but Macario found that hard to believe, coming so soon after the bloody business in Bogotá. He could assume, therefore, that the gringo was bent on disrupting his business, for whatever reason. Retaliation was a fair assumption, but the motive hardly mattered.

If his adversary wanted targets, El Padrino would provide them. He would make it easy—to a point.

And when the bait was swallowed, he would gut his adversary from the inside out.

CAPTAIN RODRIGO CELEDÓN mounted broad granite steps, ignoring the salute of one young guard on duty outside the Palace of Justice. He passed between two rows of columns supporting the building's facade, crossed the internal courtyard and entered through tall guarded doors.

Authorities were taking no chances since the latest terrorist attack, with army units joining members of his own CNP to cover the Palace of Justice and Bolívar Square. The latest incident had been a trifling inconvenience, compared to the siege and massacre in 1985, but it had struck a nerve and kindled bitter memories, inspiring every organ of the state to stand on full alert.

Did that explain why he'd been summoned back within an hour after leaving for the day? Celedón wasn't sure, but a call from Cristiano Guzman's office was always cause for alarm.

Celedón had seen the deputy vice-minister in the flesh and on the television news, but they had never met. Statesmen of Guzman's status normally preferred to deal with generals and the occasional colonel, limiting their contact with the lower ranks to public ceremonial occasions.

So, it stood to reason that the call had to mean bad news.

Initially, Celedón had feared that Lieutenant Pureza was dead, but that call would have come from a subordinate. It had to be something else.

Again, bad news.

Celedón rode an elevator to the third floor and walked half the length of a wide corridor to reach Guzman's office. His knock went unanswered, so he tried the knob, felt it turn at his touch and entered, closing the door behind him.

Guzman's anteroom was smaller than Celedón had expected, furnished with institutional chairs and a receptionist's desk that was currently unoccupied. Before Celedón had a chance to explore, a door opened behind the desk and to its left, revealing the portly form of Cristiano Guzman.

"Captain Celedón?"

"Yes, sir."

"Come in, if you please."

Celedón trailed Guzman into the deputy vice-minister's inner sanctum, watched Guzman circle his desk and sit down. No invitation to be seated was forthcoming.

"Captain Celedón," Guzman began, "I am required once more to ask if you've had any contact with your Lieutenant Arcelia Pureza."

"Required, sir?"

"By urgent circumstance."

"Sir, if there's been some word—"

"There's been more killing, Captain. This time in Tolima. I have reason to suspect that your subordinate has knowledge of these murders or may be involved in them herself."

"What evidence?" Celedón asked, omitting the obligatory "sir."

"I'm not at liberty to say," Guzman replied. "Answer the question!"

"Sir, what question?"

Guzman's face was darkening. "Captain, you're ill-advised to bandy words with me. I don't play childish games with my subordinates."

"No, sir."

"So? Do you or do you not know the whereabouts of Lieutenant Pureza?"

"Sir, I do not."

"And if I disbelieve you, Captain?"

"You would be mistaken, sir."

"Explain to me once more the nature of her last assignment," Guzman ordered.

"Sir, Lieutenant Pureza met Agent Styles from the U.S. Drug Enforcement Administration for lunch, to discuss pending cases. They often had contact, as I have explained."

"And their guest? Was he also a DEA agent, Captain?"

Celedón felt his stomach churning, feared that Guzman might hear it groaning with anxiety as he prepared to lie.

"Sir, I'm aware of no third person at their meeting."

"Captain, shall I remind you of your oath? You *are* aware that lying to superiors in an official inquiry is grounds for termination *and* for prosecution?"

"I am, sir."

"Is your answer still the same?"

"It is."

"It seems we've reached a stalemate, then." Guzman leaned forward, pressed a button on his desktop intercom and said, "It's time."

Celedón turned to find a pair of soldiers entering the office. Where they'd been concealed, to reach the room so quickly, he had no idea. Both were sergeants, wearing eagle's head insignia identifying them as members of the army's Urban Counter-Terrorism Special Forces Group.

"Captain Celedón," Guzman said, "I must now inquire if you are armed."

"No, sir."

Guzman addressed the sergeants next. "Take him away," he ordered. "And report to me immediately when you have the information I require."

Simón Bolívar Park, Bogotá

"They're coming, sir."

"I can see that, Enrique," Macario told his chauffeur. "Thank you."

Headlights cut through the darkness, two vehicles rapidly approaching the point where Macario's limousine was parked.

One of the cars stopped a block short of contact, while the other proceeded, dousing its lights when it came within thirty feet of the limousine's nose.

One of Macario's bodyguards opened his door and climbed out, shielding El Padrino with his own substantial body. Macario stood behind him for a moment, then said, "Leave me to it, Yamid—but be ready if I need you."

"*Sí, Jefe.*"

A solitary figure stepped out of the other car, approaching him with empty hands.

"*Hola,* amigo," Macario said.

"We have a problem, eh?" the new arrival said.

Macario shook hands with Pirro Aznar, field commander of the AUC. Despite his status as a fugitive from justice, Aznar showed no apprehension about surfacing in downtown Bogotá.

And why should he, with El Padrino to protect him?

"Yes, a problem," Macario replied. "The problem is a god-damned gringo and a crazy lieutenant of the CNP."

"You think they are behind this business in Tolima? One North American and a CNP bitch killing thirteen of my men?"

"And mine, as well," Macario reminded Aznar. "If they didn't do it personally, they've recruited help."

"From the government?" Aznar inquired. "That makes it worse."

"It's not official," Macario said. "I've checked my eyes and ears in the Palace of Justice. They all agree that nothing of this kind is contemplated."

"So what, then?" Aznar asked.

"Some kind of rogue operation," Macario suggested. "The Americans love their black-ops bullshit."

"And a woman from the CNP cooperates? Does that make sense to you, Naldo?"

"I've considered it," Macario replied. "The Pentagon spends millions training foreign soldiers and police in covert tactics at their School of the Americas. Those officers return indebted to the gringos, predisposed to help them with illegal projects."

"Ironic, isn't it?" Aznar asked him, smiling. "The pair of us discussing illegalities?"

"Would you rather joke about it or destroy our enemies?" Macario demanded.

Aznar stubbornly refused to take offense. "I want them dead, of course," he answered. "But I remain a happy warrior."

"Really? Shit," Macario said with a sneer. "I'm only happy when I'm making money, or the blood of enemies is drying on my hands."

"Okay," Aznar said. "But before we spill their blood, we first must find them, eh? Have you done that?"

"I'm working on it," Macario said. "It won't be long. Meanwhile, I have a plan."

"What is it?" Aznar inquired.

"To give the bastards what they want."

"It seems to me they're taking it, already."

"I can make it easier," Macario replied, smiling.

"And catch them at it, I suppose?"

"We understand each other," Macario said.

"But you need more soldiers, eh?"

"Ideally, yes."

"All right, then," Aznar said. "Tell me the rest of your outstanding plan."

7

The lock was easy, for a cop's place. Jorge Serna knew it would have been easier still to just kick in the door, but the bitch lieutenant had neighbors and Serna was loath to disturb them.

At least not just yet.

If the target gave them trouble and they had to rough her up a little, even kill her, that was different. For the moment, though, he had Marquez pick the lock with tools invariably carried on his person for exactly this kind of emergency.

Serna counted thirty-seven seconds in his head, then they were in, Vallejo leading, Serna and Reyes on his heels, with Marquez riding the caboose, remembering to shut the door again.

"Arcelia?" a youngish woman's voice called from the direction of the small flat's kitchen. Still invisible, she said, "You're late. I've been here since—"

Serna guessed she was about to cite some time, but all words failed her as the woman breezed out of a hallway leading to the other rooms and found herself confronted by four SMGs.

She did the smart thing—shut her mouth and waited.

"You're not the lieutenant," Serna said, feeling his stomach drop.

The thirty-something woman shook her head, stirring a shoulder-length wave of brunette hair to life. She was slender and well-proportioned, dressed with fair style on limited means, and her face had gone nearly bone white.

"Sister," she managed at last.

Serna spit an oath. He'd made a critical—perhaps a *lethal*— error. No one had informed him that the target had a sister.

"You live here?" he asked.

"Just visiting," she answered with a tremor in her voice. "Why do you want—"

"What's your name?" Serna interrupted in a tone that made her jump a little.

"Adriana Villalobos," the trembling woman said.

"Not Pureza?"

"I am married," she answered, speaking those three words as if they mattered in her present situation, as if putting on a ring could rescue her from fate.

"Look around," Serna instructed his companions. Then, to their unwilling hostess, "Where is your sister?"

"I don't know. I came by to surprise her. Go out to a movie or something. A bad idea."

"Where can we find Arcelia?" Serna asked.

His question helped the woman find her nerve. "Out somewhere," she replied. "Who knows? I wouldn't tell you if I did."

Just then, the three searchers returned. Two shook their heads, while Reyes said, "Nothing. Except for lots of these." He grinned and held aloft a lacy see-through bra.

"So, you're a sister, eh?" Serna asked. "Not a lesbian with an itchy pussy?"

"You're a filthy pig!" she spit at him.

Serna leaped forward, punched her squarely in the face, feeling her button nose collapse. The woman dropped, sprawling before him. Several seconds passed before she gathered breath enough to sob.

"We want your sister," he said. "And we want her right now!"

"I've already told you," she sobbed. "I came to surprise her. She may be at work or out shopping. I truly don't know!"

"Then you're useless," Serna said, raising his BSM/9.

"I could use her," Marquez interjected. "I don't give a damn if she's a lesbian."

"Or if she's married," Vallejo added.

Reading their looks, the bloodied woman cringed. "No, please. You can't! I'm pregnant!"

"Not very pregnant," Serna said.

"Eight weeks. Please, do not do that! It will hurt the baby!"

"Bullets also hurt a baby," Serna answered back.

"What are we waiting for?" Reyes asked, leering.

"She's coming with us," Serna told the other three.

"Why?" Reyes challenged him.

"Because I say so."

"You say so? Did you forget you're on probation?"

"Maybe so," Serna growled. "But El Padrino told you I'm in charge of looking for the lieutenant. Disobeying me means disobeying *him*."

Still thinking with the wrong head, Vallejo said, "He'll never know the difference if we shoot you *and* this woman."

Serna let his index finger curl around the BSM/9's trigger as he answered, face and tone deadpan. "Maybe you're right, Hector. But when you go back to him empty-handed, without me or the lieutenant, what do you think he'll do?"

Vallejo thought about it, obviously didn't like the images that came to mind, and grudgingly stood down. "Okay," he said. "We do it your way. For now."

Facing the woman once again, Serna snapped, "Get up! We're going for a ride."

She cringed from him, still weeping. "Why? I cannot help you find Arcelia."

"I think you can," Serna replied. "We'll start by leaving her a note, and you can call her from the road."

"And if she doesn't answer?"

"Then," he said, "we'll find some way to pass the time."

NALDO MACARIO'S CARTEL was not concerned exclusively with drugs. While El Padrino earned the lion's share of his income from cocaine and heroin, he also dabbled in the other vices, trusting human frailty to fill his coffers on a daily basis, rain or shine. It came as no surprise to Bolan, therefore, that Macario should own a chain of brothels dedicated to the satisfaction of diverse and "special" customers.

The house in question, catering exclusively to pedophiles, stood two blocks west of Avenida Caracas in the Tunjuelito District, operating freely within three miles of Colombian National Police headquarters. Pureza couldn't say which of the brass had been paid off to leave the cesspit unmolested, only that her signed reports describing it had disappeared into a bureaucratic void.

Cruising past the stately house located in the neighborhood of Fatima, she said, "At any given time, they have fifteen to twenty children here. The youngest that I'm sure of, eight years old, the oldest, possibly thirteen."

"Kidnapped?" Bolan asked through clenched teeth.

"In some cases, presumably. It's not uncommon, though, for daughters to be sold by rural peasant families. They have too many mouths to feed, and sons are valued most. A well-dressed stranger in a shiny car arrives, explaining that his clients in the city have grown tired of waiting for the Institute of Family Welfare to approve their application for adoption. They are out of patience, but have cash to spare. A deal is made. The parents, if they care, can tell themselves the child has found a better life."

Few things in Bolan's personal experience evoked a killing urge more swiftly than abuse of children. Hands white-knuckled on the steering wheel, he made one circuit of the block and found a place to park the Pontiac.

"I'm guessing they demand a reservation," he remarked.

"Of course."

"Guess I'll just have to crash the party, then. How's their security?"

"It's been three years since I reported on the operation," she replied. "Back then, I counted three guards working seven-hour shifts. Children who cause trouble can be threatened, drugged, eliminated. Clients are…preoccupied. There's been no difficulty to my knowledge."

"Then they're overdue," the Executioner declared.

Pureza wore new clothes, acquired from a peculiar shop that served La Zona Rosa's all-night brand of clientele. She'd stayed conservative within the limits of the inventory and looked fresh enough to Bolan by the dashboard's lights.

His mind wasn't on fashion at the moment, though.

It took a concentrated force of will to dampen the rage that Bolan felt toward child molesters, even granting that their brains had somehow been miswired from birth. He had no faith in therapy, in chemical castration, or the sundry other means employed to "cure" molesters once their pathology had crossed the deadline separating fantasy from actual predation.

Still, despite the thousand-fathom depth of his contempt for active pedophiles, he hated even more the mercenary scum who catered to their twisted needs, the nominal humans who sold innocence by the pound. Some of them wouldn't see another sunrise, if the Executioner had anything to say about it.

"You can sit this one out," he suggested.

"I think not," Pureza replied.

Bolan frowned. "Suit yourself."

"Shall we simply walk up to the door?"

"Sounds like a plan," Bolan said, as he turned and rummaged in the nearest duffel for his Spectre SMG.

The weapon's double-action trigger with decocker eliminated any need for an external safety switch, while the unique four-column magazine held fifty 9 mm Parabellum cartridges. Bolan spent a moment screwing a suppressor onto the gun's threaded barrel, then tucked it beneath his light jacket.

"Ready?" he inquired.

"Ready," Pureza said. She had the shotgun ready in her lap.

"This time," Bolan said, "no one walks except the kids."

She nodded once. "Only the children. Yes."

The neighborhood was nearly silent at this hour, well past midnight. Every window of the target house was dark, no doubt from blackout curtains, but a yellow light was burning on the porch. Bolan supposed the color had been chosen to avoid attracting insects, but to him it symbolized the cowardice and rank corruption of the brothel's management.

Before Bolan could cross the street, a Rolls-Royce Phantom pulled into the driveway, dousing headlights as he nosed in toward the house. More customers arriving? Or a pickup of the night's receipts?

No matter.

"There's our ticket to the party," Bolan told Pureza, as he stepped off from the curb.

"What do you call it? Riding on the coat's tails?"

"Close enough," he said, and broke into a jog.

CAPTAIN RODRIGO CELEDÓN had no idea where he was. Before he'd left the anteroom of Guzman's office he was hooded and his hands were pinned behind his back by plastic cuffs. From there, his military guards had marched him to an elevator, rode it down to the Palace of Justice's underground garage and shoved him roughly into the trunk of a car.

The ride they took was memorable for its speed, and for Celedón's stifling discomfort, but it hadn't lasted long enough to carry them outside of Bogotá. He had soon given up counting turns the car made, and for all he knew the soldiers could have simply driven him around downtown, before returning him to their starting point.

There'd been no second elevator ride, however, and no stairs. If they'd come back to the Palace of Justice, they had to be somewhere on the basement level, where he understood that cells were kept for "special" prisoners.

Celedón's hood was not removed until the door had closed behind him in a small square room whose only furniture consisted of two wooden chairs—one bolted to the floor—and a rectangular table with folding metal legs. A hand-crank generator sat atop the table, trailing wires that terminated in a pair of rusty-looking alligator clips. The object frightened Celedón, although it came as no spectacular surprise.

Guzman had found his answers unpersuasive. It was someone else's turn to ask, more forcefully.

The sergeants sat him down, arms creaking in their sockets as the straight back of the bolted chair slipped in between them.

Within seconds, two new plastic cuffs clamped his ankles to the front legs of the chair. Celedón did not try to rock it. Even if the bolts gave way, he had nowhere to go.

Once he was seated and secured, the questions came.

"Where is your lieutenant?" the taller of the sergeants asked.

"As I told the deputy—"

The shorter soldier swung a fist into his solar plexus, driving the air out of Celedón's lungs. He would have doubled over from the pain but couldn't, with his arms held fast behind him, and the inability to move somehow increased his suffering.

"Again," the taller sergeant said. "Where is your lieutenant?"

Celedón gasped out, "I've told you—"

Three quick punches this time, hammering his ribs. There was a moment when Celedón thought that he might wet himself, but he clamped down with deadly resolve and the feeling subsided.

For the moment.

He never doubted that humiliation would accompany torture. But Celedón had never participated in such acts, much less imagined himself on the receiving end.

All this, because he'd tried to do his job.

The taller sergeant leaned in close to Celedón's face, raising his voice. "We want the woman, and we mean to have her. There is no escape for you unless you give us what we need. You will get no mercy."

Celedón believed him, but he did not have the answer they required.

"No matter what you do," he said, when he could speak again, "I cannot tell you something I don't know."

The shorter soldier spoke for the first time. "You want us to believe you have no contact with the woman? No way you can reach her in emergencies?"

"She has a pager," Celedón said. "I've tried to reach her since the bombing, but she hasn't called me back."

"Suppose she lost it, or it was damaged. How would you reach her?" the taller one asked.

"Her cell phone. I assume you have the number. All my calls go into voice mail."

"So, you want us to believe she's broken contact?" the other asked.

"It's the truth. Believe or disbelieve it, as you like."

"Forget about the telephone," the taller of the sergeants said. "We want to know what she was doing with the two Americans in the Pink Zone."

"I'm aware of only one—"

Again, the fists. This round, they struck him six or seven times, cracking a couple of his ribs. The savage pain left Celedón slumped in his seat, restrained from falling only by the plastic cuffs that bound his wrists and ankles.

"This one is very tough," the taller sergeant said. "I think we need the electricity."

The shorter sergeant fetched the hand-crank generator, set it on the concrete floor between Celedón's feet and surveyed his body.

"Where should we start?" he inquired with a slow, crooked smile.

"The captain is proud of his virility," the other said. "Start there."

The kneeling sergeant's smile grew wider. "I've always hoped to fry a captain's eggs. This should be a treat," he replied.

Tunjuelito District, Bogotá

BOLAN AND PUREZA SAT two blocks downrange, watching police remove the first of thirteen children from the brothel. Ambulances waited to receive them. Bolan counted heads, then put the Pontiac in gear.

He didn't need to stick around and count the body bags.

No adult found inside the big house had survived. None had received the full measure of suffering they warranted, but Bolan had to trust the Universe on that score. If there was a hell or some equivalent, its deepest, foulest pits would be reserved for those he'd just sent on their way.

Three guards. One hostess-housekeeper. Nine customers with all the symptoms of decadent affluence. Whether the cops had been paid off or not, the godforsaken place was closed.

"I *really* need that shower," Pureza said.

The smell of gunpowder was strong on both of them, and Bolan didn't even want to think about the other smells inside that house of pain, the things he'd seen.

Amnesia would have been a blessing. Bolan would've welcomed it with open arms. But no such luck.

The Executioner knew he would carry every detail of it with him till his dying day. He would recall those nightmare details if he ever felt a twinge of sympathy for those he tracked.

But first, hot water. And the strongest soap that he could find.

"Another safehouse?" he inquired.

Pureza nodded and gave him an address. Bolan plotted his course.

It was another smallish house, set in another mundane neighborhood. This one, she said, was called Isla del Sol. Bolan could see no island, and the sun had yet to rise, but all he cared about was washing off the day, getting a little rest before his endless war resumed.

Pureza showered first, taking her time, but there was plenty of hot water left when Bolan got his turn. He stood beneath the stinging spray and soaped himself all over, twice, before he felt a hint of being clean.

Good luck with that, he thought, then pushed it out of mind.

He nearly missed it when Pureza called his name the first time, from the living room. Twisting the tap to kill the shower's flow, he waited for a moment, listening, then heard her call again.

"Matt!"

Priorities in order, Bolan found his Glock, then wrapped a towel around his waist and met her as she reached the bathroom door. She had a cell phone open in her hand, a desolate expression on her face.

"What is it?" Bolan asked.

Pureza shook as she held out her cell phone, her eyes brimming with tears. She took a heartbeat to compose herself, then said, "I checked my messages and found one from my sister, Adriana. She was crying, then a man came on the line and… She's been taken, Matt. Kidnapped!"

"Tell me what he said, exactly."

Pureza tapped a button on the phone, then held it to her ear, translating as she listened. "If you want to see this little bitch again in one piece, bring us the American. Call back for time and place. If we don't hear from you by four o'clock, we'll send her back in pieces, starting with…with…with her baby."

Bolan found his watch and checked it. Half-past one o'clock.

"We've still got time," he said.

"Her baby," Pureza repeated. "I didn't know she was pregnant."

"You need to focus," Bolan said. "Did they provide a contact number?"

"No. The call came from my sister's phone."

"Then you can call them back."

"And tell them what?"

"That you agree, but need some time. Tell them we're out of town and you can't get me back to Bogotá until, say, five o'clock."

"They won't believe me," Pureza said.

"It's your job to sell it. And be quick about it. We've got things to do."

"What things?"

"They've raised the ante, but they still don't understand the game," Bolan replied. "They think they're holding all the cards, but it's a dead man's hand."

"I do not understand."

"Just make the call while I get dressed. We're on the road in ten. Places to go, people to see."

"But Adriana—"

"Is our top priority," Bolan confirmed, "but you won't get her back by groveling at El Padrino's feet."

She had another thought, blinking the tears away. "My parents! What if they—"

"Another reason we should hurry," Bolan said. He dropped the towel and scrambled for his clothes. To hell with modesty.

Macario had raised the ante, sure. He had an army at his back and every reason to believe that he was calling all the shots.

But he had never faced the Executioner.

And none of those who had, in other games of life and death, had lived to play their final hand.

8

Serna was tired, but knew that if he fell asleep there could be trouble. It was hard enough keeping the female hostage from his three companions while he was awake and watching them. For all Serna knew, if he dozed, they might be on her like a pack of dogs and he would face a choice of killing them or risking further wrath from El Padrino.

Not that rape was anything unusual within Macario's cartel. The man himself had been arrested twice for sexual assault during his teens, but each time had terrorized his victims and their kin into recanting accusations, dropping the charges.

Still, Serna's only link to Arcelia Pureza was her sister, presently handcuffed and weeping in the spare room of this house in the neighborhood known as La Fragua in the Antonio Nariño District. And Lieutenant Pureza was Serna's only hope of finding the damned American who had killed his team in the Pink Zone.

La Fragua means "The Forge." Serna had no idea what had been forged or manufactured in the neighborhood, nor did he give a fat rat's ass. The only thing that mattered to him was talking to the CNP lieutenant, persuading her to trade the American for her sister. And to make that work, he needed the hostage alive, more or less fit to trade.

Of course, there'd be no trade. He would arrange a meeting, bait the trap and hand the gringo to his master on a platter. Once he had secured that bastard and the CNP lieutenant, Serna didn't care what happened to the sister. Vallejo and the rest could chop her into caiman bait, for all it mattered to Serna.

When the woman's cell phone rang, a silly chirping sound, it almost made him jump. Embarrassed, Serna snatched it from the tabletop, recognized the lieutenant's number on the LED display and growled into the mouthpiece, "What is it?"

"You left a message for me," a woman's voice said. "About my sister."

"Who is this?" Serna asked. It was critical that he identified the person he was talking to.

"Arcelia Pureza," the caller replied.

"Captain in the CNP?"

"No, a lieutenant," she replied.

"Okay. You want your sister and her baby back, or not?"

"Why else would I be speaking to you?"

"Maybe you like the bad boys, eh?" Just teasing her a bit, to keep her agitation level high.

"What do you want?" she asked him, cutting through the banter.

"I want you," he said, "and your friend from the mall. The gringo."

She hesitated for a heartbeat, then replied, "I cannot speak for him."

"That's too bad," Serna told her. "Without him, you get only half of your sister, and no baby."

"Please don't harm them!"

"Meet my terms, and you can have them back without a scratch," he lied.

"All right," she said, sounding defeated. "Where and when?"

"One hour, at—"

"No way! You're in Bogotá?"

"Where else?" Serna replied.

"I—we—are in Caquetá, near San Vicente del Caguán."

"What are you doing there?" Serna demanded, while he tried to calculate the distance in his head. Two hundred miles or more, for God's sake!

"Macario had partners here," she said.

Had partners? Why the past tense? Never mind!

"All right, then. Four hours, at—"

She interrupted him again, saying, "We have to find a car, first."

"Find a car? You didn't walk down to Caquetá!"

"No, but our car has been…damaged. We need to find another one."

"Steal one!" Serna fairly shouted at her. "If you don't want me to cut your sister's—"

"We can be in Bogotá by six o'clock," she cut into his threat. "I'm sure of it!"

"Fine," he agreed. "And not a minute later! Bring your gringo and yourself to the Park of the Martyrs. If I see one police car, your sister is dead."

"I have more to fear from the police than you do," she replied. "Park of the Martyrs. Six o'clock."

"Or else," he said.

She beat him to the disconnect, but that was fine. Serna had made his point and laid his snare. By breakfast time, he'd have a gift for El Padrino and his record would be cleansed.

It crossed his mind that he should phone and warn Macario about the danger in Caquetá, but the woman's words led him to think the damage had been done. Why should he raise more doubts about himself in El Padrino's mind? Let someone else deliver the bad news.

"Jorge!"

He turned, found Vallejo watching him. "What do you want? You let us have the woman now, eh?"

"I've said she's not for you," Serna replied, resting a hand on his BSM/9 submachine gun for emphasis. "Don't make me tell you again."

"Okay, Jorge. A joke, eh? Be cool."

"Just remember," Serna said. "You ruin this plan, and you'll wish you had never been born."

DRIVING ACROSS TOWN TO a neighborhood called Prado Veraniego in the Suba District of Bogotá, Bolan tried to brace Pureza for the possibility that something might have happened to her parents. There had been no mention of them in her conversation with Macario's soldier, but that didn't mean a hit team wasn't on the way to visit them.

Why not?

It seemed that El Padrino's men had stumbled on Pureza's sister accidentally, while checking out the lieutenant's flat, but Bolan understood the predatory mind-set. Latin drug cartels were globally notorious for their scorched-earth approach to payback. Anyone who crossed them could expect to see his or her family and friends cut down in wholesale lots, as an example to potential future enemies.

"They're fine, for the time being," Pureza said, when she got off the phone. "I told my father he must not let anyone inside the house. Just hurry, please!"

He hurried, driving crosstown on the Avenida de las Americas, then turning southward on Avenida Ciudad de Quito until he hit Ferrocami de Occidente and followed its wide loop into Prado Veranicgo. Then it was down to Pureza, telling him which way to go. Past the Colombian National Museum, their path took on a new identity, becoming Mariscal Sucre.

From there, Pureza directed Bolan through a maze of residential streets until she found the one she sought. "Ahead there, on the left," she said. "The blue house. There's a space in front."

"Let's not be hasty," he replied. "A trip around the block won't hurt."

"You think they're watching? Waiting for us?"

"I would be. Look sharp and sing out if you notice anything."

He cleared the block at normal speed, scanning along the west side, while Pureza checked the east. Bolan saw nothing that screamed "ambush," but he knew that didn't mean that they were in the clear. One of the cars parked curbside could be loaded with remote-control explosives, or there could be shooters hiding in the bushes anywhere along the quiet street.

As they began their second pass Pureza said, "We can't keep driving by like this. I need to go inside."

"Okay," Bolan said, as he pulled in to the curb. "But take the SMG. I'll cover you from here."

"You aren't coming inside?" she asked, sounding surprised.

He countered with a question of his own. "You think a gringo in the living room will help you sell this thing? They have a lot to swallow in a hurry, as it is. No point in making things more difficult."

He didn't state the obvious—that if they *were* under surveillance, it could be a fatal error to walk off and leave their car unattended. Or likewise, that if both of them were shut inside the house, no one could watch the street.

"All right, I'll be fast," Pureza said, picking up the Spectre SMG with a fresh magazine in place. "They can be stubborn, though."

"That's where you get it, I suppose."

Ignoring that, she said, "I hate to tell them about Adriana."

"Don't," Bolan replied. "At least, don't mention her until they're in the car."

"They'll blame me for it. And they should."

"Try blaming El Padrino," Bolan said. "He gave the orders."

"And I'll see him dead for that," she answered.

"First things first." He nodded toward the house. "Focus on keeping them alive."

She nodded, stepped out of the car without another word and crossed the street with long, brisk strides. Bolan kept sharp eyes on the shadows, cradling his M-4 carbine with the safety off, his finger indexed at the trigger guard.

Nothing appeared to move, but Bolan couldn't let himself relax. A sniper lurking in the night could kill with no warning except a muzzle flash, and by the time Bolan reacted it would be too late. A lesser warrior might have been relieved to see Pureza reach the porch alive, but even that could be a twist of strategy. If gunmen were in place, why not lie back and wait until she reappeared with relatives in tow, then spray the family with automatic fire?

The Executioner sat waiting, every sense alert and sampling the silent night.

Museo Nacional de Colombia, Bogotá

CRISTIANO GUZMAN WAS ADMIRING a brown, shriveled mummy, while sipping a mojito and enjoying the attention of a wealthy and well-endowed ingenue, when the cell phone on his hip began to vibrate. At first, he was determined to ignore it, but the damned thing kept on shivering against his flank like some demented insect.

Finally, smiling, he said, "I will be only a moment."

"No rest for an important man," the woman replied, making no move to step away.

"Hello," he said into the phone, without a hint of warmth.

"He is dead!" a male voice said on the other end.

Fixing his smile in place, Guzman half turned from his new friend. Instead of asking who was dead, or why, he stuck to basics. "Who is this?"

"Sergeant Alvaro Davila, sir. I am calling about—"

"Yes, yes, enough said." Was the sergeant a fool? Did he have no idea how easily cell phone transmissions could be intercepted?

"I'm sorry, sir."

"No apologies required," Guzman replied magnanimously. "When, um, did this happen?"

"Half an hour, sir, more or less."

"I see. And was the conversation…informative?"

"He was very resistant, sir. Near the end of our…discussion he admitted sending the lieutenant on a special mission, but he… left…without providing any further details."

"Shit!" Guzman caught himself, turned back to his companion with a warm, apologetic smile. "Poor help we have, these days," he said, by way of explanation.

"That's true," she granted.

"Sir? What help?" the sergeant asked.

"Never mind. What will you do, with the…package?"

"Anything you wish. Sometimes these things get lost. They disappear forever. Others are retrieved and laid to rest with pomp and circumstance."

"In this case," Guzman said, "there is no cause for celebration."

"It shall disappear," said Davila.

"Beyond all doubt?" Guzman inquired.

"You may be certain of it, sir. We are professionals."

Right, Guzman thought. Professionals who can't keep one man alive long enough to get the answers I need.

"Good," he said. "No more mistakes."

The sergeant might have offered him another apology, but Guzman didn't wait for it. Instead, he faced the young woman who would almost certainly have shared his bed this night, and offered up his own excuses.

"Alas, duty calls. I must leave you," he said, well pleased with her pouting expression of disappointment.

"So soon?"

"As you said, there's no rest for—"

"An important man," she said, completing the thought. A lacquered fingernail traced the line of Guzman's lapel. "Perhaps, if you have time within the next few days, you might call me at home?"

"Be certain of it," Guzman said.

"I haven't given you my number yet," she said, teasing.

"I'll find it," Guzman said. "No one eludes the Ministry of Justice."

"Would you take me into custody?" she fairly purred.

"Perhaps, if you've been wicked."

"Just a little."

"It may require prolonged, in-depth investigation," Guzman said.

"I'm looking forward to it," she replied. "Good night, Cristiano…and pleasant dreams."

Guzman was halfway to the nearest exit when he raised Quintaro on the phone. Another risk, but unavoidable.

"What have you learned?" Quintaro asked, with no pretense of pleasantry.

"The subject proved less durable than I had hoped," Guzman replied. "He said something about a 'special mission,' but the men whom I assigned got no details. Nothing to help us."

"As to that," Quintaro said, "I have good news."

"Ah, yes? What is it?" Guzman asked.

"My people know their job better than yours, it seems. They've found something of value to your lieutenant. An exchange is scheduled for the morning."

"An exchange? Is that wise?"

"To be made on our terms," Quintaro said, as if he were explaining to a child.

"Oh. Yes. Of course." Guzman felt silly and hated it. He wished that there was some way he could pay Quintaro back in kind, but that would be too dangerous.

Someday, perhaps, if El Padrino's lackey fell upon hard times, Guzman could seize the moment to hasten his destruction, bear in mind the countless smirking insults as he watched Quintaro squirm.

But not on this night.

"It's nearly over, then," he said, feeling relieved.

"Before long," Quintaro said, sounding confident.

"In that case," Guzman said, "good night."

He thought of going back into the party, searching out the blonde who clearly lusted after him, but Guzman kept on moving toward the exit and his waiting limousine. Having declared that he had crucial business pending, it would seem peculiar—even foolish—if he doubled back with some excuse. Tomorrow or the next day, when he called her, he could spin a tale of crises narrowly averted through his wit and wisdom.

It might even be a fair approximation of the truth.

PUREZA'S LAST AVAILABLE safehouse stood on a quiet street in the most populous neighborhood of Puente Aranda, Bogotá's sixteenth district. Her parents asked no questions on the drive from Prado Veraniego, but Bolan felt them glaring daggers at him from the Pontiac's backseat. Their eyes were hostile when he glimpsed them in the rearview mirror.

And why not?

Uprooted from their own home in the middle of the night with warnings that it was no longer safe, transported through the darkness to a strange address where they'd been cautioned not to use the telephone, open the drapes, or step outside. Who wouldn't be resentful and disturbed under those circumstances?

Bolan didn't pay much attention to most of what Pureza told her parents while in transit to the safehouse. He supposed she had to be telling them something about the threat they faced, and its connection to her job. He heard no mention of her sister's name and wondered if Pureza had decided not to share that portion of the story.

If they reached out from the safehouse, it could blow their cover, bringing cops or cartel gunmen down on top of them. And at the moment, Bolan didn't know if there was any difference between the two.

Pureza's cell phone chirped, distracting her from the conversation with her parents. It was set to warn her if she got a voice mail message, and she read the latest with a strained expression on her face.

"It's from the office," she told Bolan seconds later. "Someone that I trust. Don't look at me like that! It's just a message."

"And?"

"I mentioned Captain Celedón?"

"You did," Bolan replied.

"Two soldiers took him into custody this evening, after he was called to Cristiano Guzman's office."

"Guzman being…?"

"A deputy vice-minister with the Ministry of the Interior and Justice," Pureza replied.

"Which makes him what, in terms of rank?" Bolan asked.

"Third in command, you might say. There are several deputy vice-ministers who share—"

"I get the picture," Bolan said. "He calls your captain and has *soldiers* waiting? Not police?"

"That's right," she said. "It makes no sense, unless Guzman has reason not to trust the CNP."

"Because your captain's dirty?"

"No! I'd stake my life on that."

"You already have," Bolan said. "So maybe Guzman can't trust his own people to play along with whatever he's doing."

"Yes. That would make sense."

"I should pay him a visit."

"We have enough enemies, without tackling the government, too," she replied.

"Maybe so, if they give us a choice."

Bolan covered the street once again, while Pureza got her folks settled inside the safehouse. She was uneasy leaving them there, but arranged for a signal to reach them by phone—one ring, with a hang-up, before she called back. Otherwise, no pickups and no answering the door.

"I know it's hard to leave them," Bolan said, once they were off and rolling.

"But the safest thing," Pureza replied. "My father was a soldier, and he brought a gun, I think. My main concern at this time is to help my sister."

"You fill them in on that?" he asked.

Pureza shook her head. "I couldn't find the words," she said. "There will be time enough if we're successful. Or if not…"

"We'll get her back," Bolan said, sounding confident although he knew that nothing could be guaranteed.

"You've done this kind of thing before?" Pureza asked.

"A few times."

"And…?"

"It worked. But I'm not going to pretend that it's a lock," he added.

"Una cerradura?"

"Something certain," he explained. "We have a good chance, and the moves we make before the meet should help rattle Macario. The more men he has running around town, or pinned down guarding other sites, the fewer he can send to take us out."

"And if he kills my sister for revenge?"

"You know the bottom line," Bolan replied. "She may be dead already. All we have is some punk's promise that she'll turn up breathing for the meet. The upside is that he'll expect you to demand some proof of life before we stick our heads into the noose."

"And then he'll kill her," Pureza said.

"Then he'll *try*," Bolan said. "With any luck, he'll show up feeling overconfident, maybe shorthanded, thinking he's in charge."

"And isn't he?"

"We'll see," the Executioner replied. "He may be in for a surprise."

9

Naldo Macario felt a disturbing sense of déjà vu before he asked, "How many dead?"

"Thirteen this time," Quintaro said. "But only three of ours, plus Nina Peñalosa."

"So, the rest were customers?"

Quintaro nodded. "Yes. I have a list."

"Don't bother with the names, Esteban. How important were they?"

"One judge, a minor one. Two lawyers from a firm downtown. An aide of some kind from the Russian embassy. A professor of psychology from the national university. A football player from Unión Magdalena. A banker. An actress from the television. And you'll like this one." Quintaro beamed. "A major from the army's Brigada Antinarcoticos."

"I'm not surprised," Macario replied. "These hypocrites can't survive without the services we offer, but they still condemn us for providing them."

"We have them all on video," Quintaro said. "It's standard, as you know, in case we ever need the leverage."

"Send copies to the army, to the university and to the TV network right away. They'll help us bury this to save their own damned reputations."

"Yes, Naldo."

"As for tapes, do we have any showing the attack itself?"

"Unfortunately, no. The system was disabled from outside, somehow. I don't have details yet, with the police still—"

"So we still have no clear vision of the Yanqui. Tall, dark hair. He could be anyone."

"We have the lead from Jorge Serna."

"Possibly," Macario replied. "He's claiming contact with the lieutenant from the CNP, correct?"

"That's right. He has her sister, and the woman has agreed to meet him."

"With her friend?"

Quintaro shrugged. "So Jorge says. It doesn't mean she'll bring him, or that Serna's man enough to take him if she does."

"He hasn't asked for help with that?"

"Not yet," Quintaro said. "He wants to prove himself to you, Naldo."

"I don't care if he's macho," Macario said. "I want the job done properly, with no goddamned mistakes. Where are they meeting?"

"At the Park of the Martyrs," Quintaro said. "Six o'clock."

"Send Omar Vargas to the park with reinforcements. Have them all in place an hour early. Keep them out of sight until Omar is sure they have the woman *and* her friend."

"What should I tell Serna?"

"Tell him nothing. If he's agitated, he may spoil it."

"Naldo, what if he mistakes our men for soldiers on the other side?"

"If he attempts to interfere in any way, kill him," Macario replied.

"So be it."

"How did Serna pick the meeting time?" Macario inquired. "Why wait till six o'clock?"

"The woman told him she was in Caquetá, at San Vicente del Caguán."

"For what?"

"Hunting our partners, so she said."

"Partners? In San Vicente del Caguán?"

"Unless Jorge misunderstood her," Quintaro said.

"What sense does that make, when we have no partners there?" Macario demanded.

"Jorge would not know that."

"But *you* do, Esteban! Why would she lie?"

Quintaro shrugged. "To throw us off her trail? If we sent soldiers to Caquetá—"

"No!" Macario slammed a fist down on the desktop. "For time! She's buying time, while Serna sits and waits."

"But time for what?" Quintaro asked.

"Exactly! That's the question that you should have asked immediately, Esteban. We need to find out what they're planning and be ready for it, when it happens."

"Naldo, I can't read their minds."

"Then use your own! Remember what they've done already. Think ahead as *they* would think. Where will they hit us next?"

"There's been no pattern," Quintaro said. "First, the cocaine lab, and then the brothel."

"So? What does that tell you?"

Looking vaguely dazed, Quintaro spread his hands. "Naldo, I don't—?"

"It tells us that they may strike anywhere! We must suspend all nonessential operations this instant. Double the security on any sites we can't afford to close until this matter is resolved."

"All sites in Bogotá?"

"The cocaine lab was in Tolima, Esteban. Have you forgotten that already?"

"No, Naldo."

"Then do as I have said and double guards on *every* operation that we can't afford to close. Understand?"

"Yes."

Another second passed before Macario exploded. "Well? What are you waiting for? Go do your fucking job!"

Quintaro fled the office, leaving El Padrino with the knowledge that he might have made an enemy. It helped that there had been no other witnesses to his subordinate's humiliation, but his personality was such that he'd bear watching in the future.

Or it might be easier to simply make him disappear, when this unpleasantness had been resolved. He wouldn't be the first lieutenant whom Macario had buried in his rise to wealth and power.

Nor, Macario suspected, would he be the last.

The airstrip lay outside of Villa Isabel, a southern suburb in the Usme District of Bogotá. On paper it was owned by something called Usminia Unida Limited, one of a hundred corporations run by front men for Naldo Macario. The field's sole purpose was to transport and receive whatever El Padrino bought or sold—including drugs, black market weapons, human cargo, or selected luxuries imported for his personal amusement.

And this morning, in the darkness prior to sunrise, it was going out of business.

Bolan parked and killed his headlights when the Pontiac G6 was still a mile out from the landing field, then left the car a quarter-mile short of his goal. No camouflage was necessary in the open countryside, but he had donned a black windbreaker for the hike, while Pureza went with a charcoal-gray hoodie. She took the Benelli 12-gauge; Bolan, his M-4. Suppressors were superfluous for what he had in mind.

Scorched earth.

The airstrip was dark, but a pale quarter moon showed Bolan three planes on the ground, ranged before a fair-sized building that would double as control tower and maintenance garage. A jet-black Lincoln Navigator sat beside the building. Dim lights from within suggested that the structure was occupied.

By whom?

Identifying targets was his first priority. Bolan approached from the bungalow's blind side, scanning left and right for any signs of movement on the field, trusting Pureza to double-check the ground. When no one opened fire or called for them to halt, he crept around the building to the nearest window, paused, then risked a look inside.

He found three swarthy soldiers playing cards around a standard metal desk, identical to those he'd seen in schools and lower-budget offices around the world. The only decorations in the place were maps tacked to the walls. No pesos had been spent to make this house a home.

All three of the cardplayers wore sidearms, and they had automatic weapons planted here and there, within arm's reach. Security, no doubt, but it was just as clear they didn't take the mission seriously. They'd assigned no one to watch and wait outside.

Strike one.

The last thing Bolan noted on his visual recon was that they'd left the building's one and only door wide-open to the night, presumably so they could hear if anyone approached. It made sense, to a point, but obviously they were counting on a noisy vehicle to tip them off, rather than infiltrators creeping up on foot.

Strike two.

He signaled for Pureza to remain in place beside the window, while he edged around the bungalow to reach the open door. Bolan heard the gamblers kibitzing and laughing, negating any benefit they might have garnered from the open door.

Strike three.

He stepped into the doorway, M-4 carbine at his shoulder, with the fire-selector switch set for 3-round bursts. The soldier facing Bolan from the far side of the desk glanced up and saw him, dropped his cards and died before he had a chance to speak.

The first shots roused his comrades, sent them breaking off to right and left, respectively. Bolan took down the nearer of them with a triple-tap between the shoulder blades, and he was swinging toward the third when Pureza joined the fight, firing through the window with her 12-gauge for the kill.

Three up, three down.

Which left the planes.

The first was a Learjet 40-XR, with seats for seven passengers and a two-member crew. The second was a Piper PA-46 Malibu, a single-pilot prop aircraft that could carry five passengers or

4,100 pounds of cargo. The last was a workhorse: the Cessna 208 Caravan turboprop built to haul nine thousand pounds of cargo over "short" hauls.

The total price tag for Macario's three planes: a cool twelve million dollars, retail.

Bolan made short work of them. First he retrieved a box of flares and some old rags from the maintenance shed, then circled the aircraft, removing each plane's fuel cap in turn. Each vent received an uncapped flare swaddled in cloth to hold it steady. When all three planes had been primed, he lit a fourth flare and made the rounds a second time, like an Olympic torchbearer, lighting each of the fixed flares in turn.

And then, he ran like hell.

Bolan and Pureza were a hundred yards beyond the airstrip's control shack when the first plane blew. The other two were close behind, fuel tanks erupting into oily fireballs reaching for the sky. Bolan imagined he could feel twelve million dollars burning in the night, lighting his way back to the Pontiac.

And toward the next target on his roster.

Carrying the fire.

THEY HAD RETURNED TO Chapinero Central where it all began, barely a half day earlier, in the financial center of the capital. Pureza felt exposed there, knowing she was hunted by Macario's cartel, by her own department and perhaps by the army, as well.

If Deputy Vice-Minister Guzman was using soldiers to interrogate her captain, then it followed that the same men or others like them would be tracking her. She couldn't guess what Captain Celedón might tell them under torture, but he could not give the enemy her whereabouts or tell them where she might strike next.

The enemy.

For years, since her recruitment by the CNP, Pureza had been a part of Colombia's law enforcement system. It had puzzled her at times, shamed her on various occasions, but she'd never thought of other officers within the same milieu as enemies.

Until this day.

She pushed that troubling thought away as they approached their target, rolling eastward on Calle 56 toward a T-intersection with Calle 13. A short jog north from there, then east again on Calle 56A and Cooper steered the Pontiac into the parking lot behind a block-long office complex.

"This is it?" he asked, confirming their arrival.

"*Sí*. Macario's office suite is on the fourth floor, at the southeast corner."

"Great," Bolan said. "Time to drop in and pay our respects."

"I should be looking for my sister."

"Where?" the big American asked. "Going door-to-door in Bogotá and asking seven million people if they've seen her?"

"I could ask Macario himself," she answered.

"He's already sending her to us. At six o'clock."

"And what will she have suffered in the meantime?" Pureza asked.

"Nothing you could prevent," he replied. "It's all Macario's responsibility, not yours."

"And yet, if not for me—my choice of jobs, my running off with you, Cooper, she would be safe."

"Nobody's safe with Macario breathing," he said. "I'm following through on our plan, but you're free to bail out."

"And pretend I was kidnapped?" She laughed. "It is too late for that, when they have my captain."

"Take your parents and run," he said. "I've got cash for the first leg. Get out of the city. Find someplace to hide. My people can toss out a lifeline."

"I'm coming with you," she replied. "For my sister."

"Then let's get a move on," he said, stepping out of the car.

They left most of their weapons in the Pontiac, each carrying a hidden sidearm, Bolan with grenades clipped to his belt beneath his jacket. Thermite, as he'd explained to her, for starting fires that water could not quell.

There was a plainclothes guard on duty in the lobby, sitting in a little booth beneath a sign that offered *Información*. Before the man could ask their business, Bolan lunged across the desk and knocked him sprawling from his chair, then leaped into the booth and struck him one more time, to leave the guard unconscious.

While she watched, he bound the man's stout arms behind his back, using the guard's own belt, then pulled his shoes and socks off. He stuffed one sock into the captive's mouth and used the other one to tie the first in place, knotted behind his head.

"I'm glad he wears tube socks," Bolan said, as he left the booth.

"I hope it's a fresh pair," Pureza replied disdainfully.

No music entertained them in the elevator, riding up to the fourth floor. Presumably it was turned off at closing time and started up again each morning, as the building's tenants started to arrive. The silent ride was ominous, and the soldier drew his pistol as they neared their floor, prompting Pureza to do likewise.

All in vain.

The fourth floor was deserted, like the rest of the building around them. Even its cleaning crew had finished for the night—make that the morning—and departed to their homes. Pureza led Bolan along the hallway to Macario's door, bearing the title *Empresas Unidas* in bright gilt letters.

Pureza automatically translated. "United Enterprises."

"Nice and vague," he said, and fired a muffled shot into the dead bolt lock.

Once inside, they opened doors to the suite's several plush offices, then pulled computers from their moorings and stacked them in the middle of the reception chamber. Bolan popped the lock on one of ten or twelve black filing cabinets, primed one of his thermite canisters and placed it in an open drawer. Retreating to the front, he rolled a second grenade against the stack of computers.

"Time to go," he told Pureza.

And they ran.

The guard was stirring in his booth when they reached the lobby. Bolan stopped to untie him but left him to deal with the gag on his own.

A moment later they were rolling in the Pontiac, Pureza feeling her excitement start to ebb, replaced once more by worry for her sister.

Soon they would be together. Soon she would hold Adriana in her arms.

If they lived that long.

DESPITE HIS GIVEN NAME, Cristiano Guzman was not a religious man. Normally he attended church only for weddings and funerals, the latter occasions becoming more frequent with age. The last thing he would do, on any normal day, was drive to a cathedral in the heart of Bogotá and make a show of praying.

But, of course, this was no normal day.

He had been summoned once again by Esteban Quintaro, this time to the Church of Our Lady of Lourdes. The house of worship was open all night, with a lone security guard to prevent vandalism or theft. The guard—a dumpy little man dressed in a wrinkled uniform of sorts—ignored Guzman when he arrived, rightly deciding that a sneak thief would not wear an expensive suit.

Quintaro had arrived before him. Guzman spied him in a pew halfway between the narthex and the altar, on his left. Crossing the sanctuary, Guzman felt like an impostor trespassing in God's house on unholy business. Still, if God existed anywhere outside the mind of man, He had to know that Guzman had no choice.

A moment later he was seated in Quintaro's row, careful to leave a half arm's length between them. Rubbing shoulders would have been too much, the ultimate indignity.

"Progress?" Quintaro asked.

"Sadly, nothing has changed or come to my attention since our last conversation," Guzman replied.

"Hmph. Each time we meet," Quintaro said, "you disappoint me more and more."

Guzman tried to suppress the tremor in his voice as he replied. "Clearly, my wish is not to disappoint," he said. "I have—"

"Clearly?" Quintaro interrupted him. "It isn't clear to me at all. I promise you it is not clear to El Padrino."

Sensing that his life could end at any instant, Guzman asked, "What more can I possibly do?"

Quintaro turned and pinned him with a glare. "As I've previously mentioned, I have a plan to draw your lieutenant out of hiding," he replied. "But if it fails, I need your whole department mobilized to find her without any more delays. Someone among your officers must know her well enough to plot her movements."

"Absolutely! They are searching for her as we speak."

"As for the Yanqui who is with her, someone at your ministry must know his name or who he represents," Quintaro said. "It's unbelievable that Washington would reach out to a lowly captain in Bogotá, bypassing all higher authority. Find out who asked the gringos for assistance and we'll question him ourselves."

"It could be anyone," Guzman replied. "Even the President!"

"Presidents are only mortal men," Quintaro said. "Like you and I."

Guzman recoiled from the suggestion that the leader of his nation might be marked for death by El Padrino, but he felt no great surprise. Over a quarter century in Bogotá, cartels had slaughtered half of Colombia's Supreme Court justices, along with countless prosecutors and policemen, union leaders, journalists and critics of the cocaine trade. Car bombings had become almost routine. What would restrain Macario from an attack upon the nation's highest elected official?

"I'll get the information somehow," Guzman promised.

"For your own sake, Cristiano. Maybe you should say a prayer before you leave?"

"God doesn't listen to me," Guzman said.

"In that case," Quintaro said, "good luck."

Guzman nodded, rising.

He would need good luck, in order to survive.

10

"The airstrip *and* my office! Do you hear me, Esteban?"

Macario was pacing in his study, fists clenched, teeth bared, a vein on his forehead pulsing visibly. To Quintaro he resembled an attack dog on a chain, at feeding time.

"I hear you, Naldo," Quintaro replied.

What else could he say? He already knew what was coming. The only question that remained in his mind was whether he'd survive the next half hour in one piece.

"You've failed me yet again! Can you explain how this keeps happening?"

"Please, Naldo. If you recall, guards were withdrawn from some locations on your order, to increase security at other places."

"So, you're blaming *me* for this disaster? Is that what you're saying?"

"Of course not. No one could predict where these crazy bastards may appear at any moment."

"But I pay you to predict such things," Macario hissed, as he made another pass across the room. "*You* are supposed to anticipate our enemies' movements and crush them, understand?"

"Yes, but—"

"Yet you fail me, time and time again! Why was the airstrip not protected? Will you claim I told you to withdraw the guards?"

"No. There were three guards at the field," Quintaro said.

"All dead, and my planes destroyed! Millions of dollars left in ashes! Transport of our products paralyzed!"

"Naldo, we have more planes to—"

"That's besides the point! Three men were not enough! These people kill ten or fifteen at a time, as if it's nothing. How could three men ever hope to stop them?"

"If they'd been alert—"

"You chose them, Esteban! If they were sleeping on the job, whose fault is that?"

"Naldo, I didn't say—"

"And then my office! All the files and our computer records gone like that!"

Quintaro flinched at the snap of Macario's fingers, then said, "We discussed the office, you remember? No guards, we said, because the building has its own security."

"Which obviously counts for nothing, eh?" Macario replied, starting another pass by the spot where Quintaro stood rigid. "I want these so-called guards identified today! I want them dead! I want their goddamned useless eyes brought here to me! Do you understand?"

"Yes, Naldo." If Quintaro had a mission, it could only mean that he would be alive, and yet…

"How goes the plan to trap these devils?"

Glancing at his watch, Quintaro said, "The meeting has been set for six o'clock. Our reinforcements are in place. As we agreed, Jorge was not informed of the assistance we're providing."

"If this fails, Esteban, if you let me down again…"

"It will not fail, Naldo." Suddenly, Quintaro blurted out, "I plan to lead the reinforcements personally."

"Ah. Hands-on this time, is it?"

"For best results."

Macario allowed himself a thin-lipped smile. "In that case," he replied, "I won't detain you any longer. Go and make me proud."

BOLAN DROVE NORTH ALONG Avenida Caracas, which separated Los Mártires from the district of Santa Fe to the east, approaching its intersection with Calle 10. His mind was on the immediate future, while Pureza briefed him on her country's past.

The district and its central park were named the Park of the Martyrs after five freedom fighters who'd been executed on the spot by Spanish troops during the early nineteenth century. Bolan couldn't say whether Macario had any sense of irony, but his selection of a meeting place—an ambush site—suggested that he might.

"We're early," Pureza said.

"They will be, too," Bolan replied. "Setting a trap takes time."

"Do you believe they will bring Adriana?"

Although far from positive, he answered, "I don't see why not. They know you'll ask to see her."

"But she may be dead."

"We'll handle it, whatever happens," Bolan said.

"I know. I must prepare myself."

"That's what we're doing," he said, skirting the park with other early-morning traffic. El Padrino's kidnappers had picked a public place, but there would be no strollers at this hour. Most shops and offices in Dogotá opened their doors between nine and ten o'clock. Rush hour would begin sometime between eight and eight-thirty.

By that time, the bodies would be hauled away or cooling on the ground.

With any luck, the Executioner's wouldn't be among them.

Vans and other vehicles were parked at intervals around the park and on its side streets. Bolan couldn't see inside them, for the most part, and he couldn't guess how many shooters might be tucked away in nearby buildings—say, the lobby of that tall apartment building, or the newsagent's three doors down the street. Guns could be anywhere and everywhere around him, but he had to take the bait.

Full daylight wouldn't break on the Park of the Martyrs for ninety minutes yet, which granted him some cover for the first approach. There would be light enough for fighting from the lampposts set around the park and floodlights on the central obelisk, once Adriana's captors showed themselves, drawing Pureza and Bolan into killing range.

"I want to thank you, while there is time," Pureza said, "for helping me."

"It's why I'm here," Bolan replied, thinking the woman and her kinfolk would be better off if they had never met.

"I know," she said. "That's why I thank you."

Bolan found a spot to park the Pontiac, a half block north of the park. Observed by hostile eyes? He didn't know, and couldn't help it, either way.

"Let's have a closer look," he said, and pocketed the keys, reaching behind him for the nearest duffel bag.

"YOUR SISTER WILL BE coming soon," Jorge Serna informed his prisoner. Although they were secure inside the Toyota 4Runner SUV, he kept his voice low-pitched.

"You may regret it when she does," the handcuffed woman answered.

Serna smiled at that. "Your optimism does you credit," he replied. "You are brave."

"My sister's brave, not me," she said.

"We'll find out soon enough," he said, stroking the BSM/9 submachine gun in his lap.

A quick glance at his watch told Serna it was nearly time. He took the little walkie-talkie from his pocket, keyed it and spoke into the early-morning darkness.

"Hector! Manuel! Are you ready?"

"Yes, I'm ready," Manuel Reyes answered back.

Hector Vallejo agreed.

Serna had staked them out to cover the park from its corners, Reyes at the northwest, Vallejo at the southeast, while he and Fernando Marquez waited with the woman in their van, on the southwest. It left one corner unguarded, but Serna wanted Marquez at the van's wheel when the action started, ready to follow and cut off their targets if either was still moving after the first fusillade.

"Come with me," he commanded, clutching his hostage's arm as he opened the van's left rear door. Serna had access to the SMG, suspended on a harness underneath his coat, through a slit pocket on the right.

"This way," he said, steering Adriana Villalobos toward the obelisk commemorating valiant deaths in ancient times. Where better for the fresh blood of his adversaries to be spilled?

He stopped her short beside the obelisk, in plain view from all sides. "A big smile for your sister. Let her know how pleased you'll be to see her face again."

He didn't check to see if she obeyed. The smile would be superfluous. It was the woman, on her feet and breathing, who would draw the lieutenant to her death.

Then he saw someone approaching slowly, from the north side of the park. A solitary figure, obviously female, hands stuffed in the pockets of a knee-length coat. The features were obscured, but Serna half imagined he could feel the new arrival's eyes bore into him.

But where was her gringo companion?

"Stop there!" he called out, when she'd closed the gap by half.

"I've come as you requested," she replied in a steady voice.

"But only one of you is here," Serna replied. "Where is the Yanqui?"

"Don't you see him?" the lieutenant asked. "He sees you."

Before Serna could answer, something slammed into his forehead, pitched him over backward and his vision of the world winked out.

BOLAN'S CHOICE FOR DISTANCE shooting was a Heckler & Koch PSG-1 semiautomatic rifle chambered in 7.62 mm NATO rounds, feeding a 20-round box magazine. The rounds would travel 2,848 feet per second, with an effective range of almost 900 yards. The weapon's Hendsoldt ZF6x42PSG-1 telescopic sight with illuminated reticle gave Bolan all the visual enhancement he required.

He scanned the Park of the Martyrs from a rooftop to the west, his view of the tableau completely unobstructed. So far, he had spotted only three shooters afoot and one remaining in the SUV that had dropped off Pureza's sister and her watchdog. Bolan tracked them to the obelisk, waiting.

Pureza showed herself, as planned, slowly approaching.

"Stop there!" the obelisk shooter called out, seconds later.

"I've come as you requested," Pureza said.

"But only one of you is here," the gunman said. "Where is the Yanqui?"

"Don't you see him?" Pureza replied. "He sees you."

Bolan took the head shot, knowing it was clean before the trigger broke. The dead man tottered on his heels for half a second, wore a halo glinting crimson in the lights that flanked the obelisk, then crumpled to the flagstones.

Adriana froze, dropped to one knee, a sensible enough reaction in the circumstances. As the echo of his gunshot rolled away and Bolan swiveled toward his second mark, Pureza cried out to her sister, "Adriana! Run to me!"

And Adriana ran, as if her life depended on it, which was true enough.

An automatic weapon stuttered from the southeast corner of the park, a muzzle flash in motion as the gunner started to pursue Pureza. He managed six or seven strides before the second round from Bolan's PSG-1 ripped into his chest and lifted him completely off his feet. He hit the pavement on his back and started twitching through his death throes in a spreading pool of blood.

An engine's roar brought Bolan's weapon sweeping back toward the Toyota SUV that had delivered Adriana to the killing ground. He couldn't see its driver through the tinted glass, but knew exactly where the guy was sitting all the same.

His third shot drilled the 4Runner's windshield without losing any significant speed. In case the gunman in the driver's seat was only wounded, Bolan sent another round downrange to finish him and saw the SUV wander off course, meandering until it struck a mailbox at the curb.

One shooter was still in view and spraying automatic fire toward the retreating women. Bolan swung his rifle toward the northeast corner of the park, to finish it—and then all hell broke loose.

QUINTARO HAD NOT BEEN entirely truthful when he promised El Padrino that he'd lead the reinforcements when they closed their trap at the Park of the Martyrs. What general in history was fool enough to lead a charge through hostile fire and lived to tell the tale?

Quintaro would *direct* the action safely, from a distance, and the victory would still be his. He would erase whatever doubts Macario might have concerning his ability to lead the family and crush its enemies.

Unless, of course, he failed.

Quintaro saw the lieutenant they'd been hunting surface from the shadows and approach the obelisk where Serna held her sister in the glare of floodlights. There was no sign of a male companion yet, but he would doubtless be observing from the nearby darkness, where Quintaro's men would spot him when he made his move.

And there it was! A puff of blood from Serna's head, and he went down. A rifle shot that echoed over the park, and then Quintaro saw the set begin to fall apart.

The captive woman ran toward her sister, gaining ground, while one of Serna's backup soldiers opened fire. He missed, began pursuing them, then tumbled as a second rifle shot rang out.

Where was the goddamned sniper?

Groping for his two-way radio, Quintaro saw Serna's black SUV lurch into motion, clearly bent on running down the women, but a one-two punch from the invisible rifleman took out its driver and left the Toyota adrift, looping harmlessly off toward the curb.

Quintaro found the radio, keyed it and shouted to his waiting troops, "Attack! Stop the woman! Find the sniper!"

What more could he offer? It was all common sense, and the best he could do.

At once, two dozen soldiers sprang from hiding in doorways, alleys, parked cars, converging on the battleground with weapons in their hands. They had the park surrounded. It should be impossible for anyone to break their line and slip away.

But with the sniper still at work…

"You, too!" Quintaro told his driver. "Get in there and help them!"

"Yes, boss, but—"

"No buts about it, Reynaldo! Get moving!"

Instantly, Quintaro slid into the driver's seat of the Mercedes-Benz ML350 SUV. He locked the doors, then reached inside his jacket for the .357 SIG P228 pistol holstered in a shoulder rig.

And waited, with the fingers of his right hand clutching the ignition key.

PUREZA GRABBED HER SISTER'S arm, no time for the embrace she craved, and ran back toward the shadows ringing the Park of the Martyrs. Off to her right, she saw an SUV in motion, rolling on an interception course, then two more shots from Cooper's rifle changed the driver's mind, sending the vehicle off course.

"Arcelia—"

"Run! We'll talk later!" she commanded, as she drew the shotgun from beneath her long coat with her free hand.

Suddenly the air around them was alive with bullets, buzzing past from every side. Pureza ducked her head and dragged her sister by her handcuffed wrists, toward the street where the Pontiac G6 was parked.

"Arcelia!"

"Keep running!"

A man appeared in front of them, as if from nowhere, brandishing a stubby automatic weapon. On the run, Pureza fired a blast from her Benelli 12-gauge and tattooed his chest with buckshot pellets. Hearing Adriana squeal behind her, she reached back and clutched her sister's handcuffs, dragging her along before her stride could falter.

Pureza thought about the child her sister was carrying, a joyous surprise that could still turn tragic at any moment. She had two lives in her hands, with only her wits and the shotgun to save them.

And the big American's rifle, still sweeping the park.

Pureza spotted two gunmen jogging toward her from the left, one dropping to a knee and aiming at her with a submachine gun while the other rushed ahead. Before she had a chance to level her Benelli, she saw Cooper strike the kneeling shooter from his rooftop aerie, knocked him sprawling with a clean shot through the neck.

She met the runner with a shotgun blast that turned his face into a crimson smear and slammed him backward, tumbling through the air. With all the gunfire hammering around her, somehow, she still heard the clinking impact of her 12-gauge cartridge on the flagstones to her right.

Running.

It seemed as if the race with death would never end. As if in a dream, Pureza had a sense that she was trapped in place, expending her last ounce of energy without a trace of progress. Any second a shot could find her and she'd tumble to the pavement, leaving Adriana and her unborn child alone in the cross fire.

But then, the sprawl of the park was suddenly behind them. They had reached the nearest street and crossed it, bullets pinging off the pavement at their heels. Pureza spun and fired a parting blast at her pursuers, letting Adriana pull ahead, then turned once more and followed her sister into darkness.

Into fragile safety of a sort, if they could only reach the car.

BOLAN COVERED THEIR RETREAT, taking his pick of targets from the roof, dropping one magazine when it was empty, instantly replacing it to start again.

There'd been no time to count the soldiers ducking, dodging, running willy-nilly through the park and streets below him. All that mattered, for the moment, was diverting shooters from Pureza's trail. She had keys to the Pontiac, could take her sister and escape if things went south for him, but she would wait a little while.

Which meant that it was time for him to move.

But first…

Three gunmen reached their fallen comrade at the obelisk. One bent to check his head wound, while the others stood with backs turned to the corpse, looking for targets on the ground.

Tracking from left to right, the Executioner dropped all three. Part of the craft was muscle memory, long years of training and experience that told him when the PSG-1's stock was wedged against his cheek and shoulder perfectly, its barrel steady, telescopic sight aligned for maximum effect. The rest was down to expert skill, three shots in something close to rapid fire from eighty yards, and three men down.

How many left?

It wasn't Bolan's mission to annihilate the enemy this time. His goal had been removal of Pureza's sister from the cartel's clutches, with a lesson sent back to Macario besides.

But if he had to drop them all, he would.

Bolan had dropped eleven of the late arrivals when the field below him cleared. One of the reinforcements who was still alive and kicking had him spotted, trying to duel from a hundred yards out with a submachine gun, his rounds falling short to pepper the building's facade several floors below Bolan.

It wasn't much of a challenge, but Bolan took time to respond, lining up on the SMG's muzzle flash, firing one round for effect that ripped into the weapon and probably fractured the shoulder behind it. His challenger dropped out of sight, concealed by a four-door sedan at the curb, and stayed there.

Wounded? Dazed? Bolan didn't much care.

He was up, then, and moving before any other contenders weighed in from below. The Executioner crossed the roof in a sprint to a fire escape on the north wall, leading down to an alley and onward from there to the street.

Pureza had the G6 running by the time he reached it, with

her sister slumped in the shotgun seat. Bolan piled in behind them, and the Pontiac was off before he had a chance to shut his door.

"She's fine," Pureza said, not waiting for the question.

Bolan watched the lights of the park dwindle behind them, wondering if that was true. She was *alive,* at least. And maybe, for the moment, that was good enough.

11

Ciudad Montes, Bogotá

Job one, after they'd put a safe distance between themselves and the Park of the Martyrs, was getting Adriana out of the handcuffs. Thankfully, Pureza had her own cuff key, which did the trick.

Job two was putting in a call to Adriana's husband, who'd been on the verge of filing a police report when he came home to find her missing and could not contact Pureza or their parents. He was presently en route to meet them at the safehouse where his in-laws waited, with a stern warning to tell no one where he was going.

"They might follow him," Pureza said to Bolan.

"Possible," he granted, "but there wasn't any point in telling him to watch for tails. He won't know what to look for and he likely couldn't ditch them, anyway."

"Who were those people?" Adriana asked her sister from the backseat. "All this time, they wouldn't tell me anything."

"They were drug traffickers," Pureza said. "Terrorists."

"Will they come after Miguel? Mom and Dad?" Adriana hovered on the brink of tears once more.

"Our parents are safe," Pureza replied. "You and Miguel will soon be joining them."

"How safe can we be, in Bogotá? I've heard you say that drug traffickers run the government!"

"Not all of it. And that may be about to change," Pureza said.

"Because the two of you will fix it? When the army and police cannot?"

Bolan could understand the woman's skepticism. And, in fact, he knew they couldn't change the system in Colombia. Uprooting the cocaine economy that had evolved over the past four decades, much less quelling the endemic violence that had rocked the country since the end of World War II, might be impossible. For two soldiers fighting alone, it was a pipe dream.

But they *could* eliminate Naldo Macario and some of those in public life who served him willingly. They'd made a start on that already, and the work was still progressing. If they simply wound up toppling El Padrino so that someone else could take his place…well, that was life.

Bolan had never claimed to be a savior.

He already had his hands full as the Executioner.

It had begun to seem habitual, his waiting in the car to guard Pureza while she settled loved ones in a home-away-from-home. Bolan didn't mind, recalling that family that had launched his lonely war so long ago. When family was threatened, some people would break and run, while others went to any lengths in its defense.

With any luck, Bolan thought, this would be the last time that Pureza would have to relocate her next of kin. If they could weather the approaching storm, they might return to normal life—whatever that meant in Colombia these days. Or, if Pureza was forced out of her job and home, perhaps they'd pull up stakes and try to start anew. Brognola might be able to assist them on that score, but it was out of Bolan's hands.

Meanwhile, he had a war in progress that required his full attention. El Padrino and the troops that still remained to him, augmented by the AUC, would be intent on payback for the bungled trap and all the other damage the cartel had suffered since the Executioner arrived in Bogotá. Without Pureza's family to push around, Macario would have a paucity of targets, but he might respond as in the past, with random acts of terrorism targeting the government or the civilian population.

To prevent that, Bolan had to keep his adversary busy dousing conflagrations in his own backyard. And in the process, there might be a way to fracture his alliance with the AUC.

The time had come, Bolan decided, to reach out and touch someone.

"IF HE'S NOT DEAD, THEN where is he? Can no one tell me that, for God's sake?"

Five men stood before Naldo Macario with shoulders hunched, their fearful eyes averted from his wrath. They were survivors of the massacre at the park. Another twenty-three were dead, and one was missing.

Esteban Quintaro.

"Well?" El Padrino shouted. "Speak to me, goddamn you!"

One of them began to raise a hand, as if he were a child in school asking to use the toilet, then he lowered it again and said, "Sir, we never saw Mr. Quintaro after he assigned us our positions. When the shooting started, well, he must have left."

"You mean he ran away?"

"We don't know. The sniper started firing—"

"Sniper? What sniper?"

"From a rooftop, sir," another of the men said. "I saw him—or the muzzle flash, at least—but he was out of range for my pistol."

"Yes, sir," a third man said. "He was taking out everyone!"

"Oh? If he was killing everyone, how did the five of you escape? Perhaps *you* ran away, and blame Esteban for your own cowardice?"

"No, sir!" the first man who had spoken said. "We were forced to duck and hide, of course, or else we would be dead and you'd have no idea what happened. But we're not cowards. The sniper slipped away after he helped the women run. We never saw him go, but stayed to help the others if we could until police arrived."

"So, you helped dead men?"

"We believed that some were still—"

"Bastard! That's enough!" Macario was livid, seething. "We must find Esteban immediately. If he's dead, police will have his body at the morgue. If he was captured by our enemies, they will make contact. But if he has run away…"

The thought sickened Macario, but he could not deny that it was possible. He'd seen men break before when faced with danger, some of them reduced to tears and wailing as if they were frightened children.

And if panic had consumed his second in command, there was a penalty that Esteban had to pay. For the desertion of his men and his godfather, he had to suffer, serving as a grim example to Macario's remaining troops. His agonizing death would be a lesson to them all.

A lesson that Macario himself would personally supervise.

But first, he had to be found. And at the same time, there were enemies to locate, identify and destroy. They had to be crushed before they undermined Macario's empire beyond repair.

"You," he said, confronting the soldier who had answered most directly to defend himself and the other survivors of the park. "I have forgotten your name."

Macario pretended that he knew the soldier's name, but simply needed a reminder of it, when in fact he wasn't sure he'd ever seen the man before.

"Santiago Villegas, sir," the man replied.

"Until such time as Esteban is found, you will replace him," Macario said. "And if it's true he ran away like a coward, you will help me to extract revenge. Do you agree?"

As if there was a choice. Of course he would agree.

"Yes, sir," Villegas said. "You honor me."

"It is an honor you must earn," Macario replied. "Beginning immediately. We have a man inside the CNP who will cooperate in your examination of the bodies from the park. If Esteban's is not among them, next make sure that he was not arrested. After that…we'll talk again."

"Yes, sir. Consider it done!"

Macario had no doubt that it would be done. His new lieutenant was not only eager to impress—he knew that one more failure meant his own inevitable death.

Pan-American Highway, Eastbound

AS ESTEBAN QUINTARO SPED eastward on the Pan-American Highway, he knew that he had to be a hunted man by now. Macario would have learned that he was not among the dead recovered by police from the park. And since he had not come home groveling to face his punishment for the disastrously bungled ambush, it could only mean that he was running.

Thankfully, Quintaro had prepared for such a day. The trunk of his Mercedes-Benz contained one suitcase filled with clothing and another stuffed with cash—bundles of 50,000-peso notes, twenty thousand in all, which would convert to about half a million U.S. dollars. It was enough to get Quintaro started in a new life, and he had another thirteen million U.S. dollars banked in Panama, unknown to El Padrino.

An escape fund, as it were.

Quintaro was a forward-looking predator. From childhood he had watched the rise and fall of drug lords, and each in turn had been eradicated, either by the law, by stronger competition or by traitors from within.

So even as he lived in splendor, counting cash and playing chess with human lives, Quintaro had prepared in secret for the day when he would have to cut and run, to save himself from the inevitable fate of those who reached too high, too fast.

Quintaro didn't know what would become of Macario and the others he had left behind, nor did he truly care. Although he'd risen to the second-highest rank within Macario's cartel, there was a distance kept between them, clearly demonstrating that equality was inconceivable. Quintaro could imagine El Padrino raging, bellowing demands that he be found, captured, delivered for dissection by Macario's pet sadists.

That search would work against Macario, diverting troops when they were badly needed to defend the family against the enemies who had been thrashing them relentlessly since the explosion in The Pink Zone. Every man pulled off the firing line to hunt Quintaro weakened the cartel and made Macario's defeat more likely.

Which was fine with Quintaro.

If his former boss was killed, the contract on his life would die with him. And if he lived, the battle should distract him long enough to let Quintaro disappear.

Where would he go?

From Panama, a whole wide world awaited him. Colombia might be too hot for years to come, but in addition to the fortune he had squirreled away, Quintaro also had three new identities awaiting him, each buttressed by the best forged birth certificates, passports and other vital documents blood money could buy. Young and handsome, fluent in Spanish and English, Quintaro believed he could live anywhere.

And he knew all of Macario's connections, from Peru, Bolivia and Panama to the United States, Canada and Europe. His name was known among leaders of the Sicilian Mafia and the French Unione Corse. A trip to Bangkok on Macario's behalf had introduced him to the so-called "mountain master" of the 14K Triad. In short, he had no dearth of opportunities.

Quintaro thought that running for his life might be the best move he had ever made.

THE NEIGHBORHOOD THAT Bolan sought was called La Amistad, which translated as "friendship." The notion almost made him smile, considering the most unfriendly nature of their mission.

Dawn had broken over Bogotá, and while a female radio announcer offered details of the massacre at the park in breathless tones, Bolan was looking for the next mark on his hit list.

This time, he was switching from Macario's cartel to El Padrino's sidekicks and defenders in the AUC—the so-called United Self-Defense Forces of Colombia. Right-wing vigilantes at best, and mercenary terrorists at worst, the AUC's guerrillas formed an integral part of Macario's defensive line. They'd chosen sides, sold out whatever principles they may have claimed in the beginning for a slice of the drug dealer's pie.

And they were going down.

"It's there," Pureza said, pointing. "Third one on the left."

Bolan drove past the storefront with its banner sign reading *La Voz de la Verdad*—The Voice of Truth—which was also the name of a weekly tabloid published by the AUC in Bogotá, regaling readers with its simplistic program for "national salvation." The platform boiled down to wholesale eradication of lawbreakers—apparently defined as anyone who didn't kowtow to the AUC.

"Looks closed," Bolan observed.

"They always have a few men here, sleeping in back. Sometimes more than a few."

A few would do it, for his present purposes. The action in La Amistad wasn't supposed to be decisive. Dub it something in the nature of a wake-up call, to rouse the AUC's brass and put their nerves on edge in advance of Bolan's next move.

His tactic was divide and conquer. This was where he'd start to hammer in the wedge.

An alley ran behind the shops and offices, three blocks west of Avenida Battalón Caldas. Bolan drove past it at a snail's pace, eyeballing its length, before he made another left-hand turn and parked the Pontiac.

"I'd like you to stay in the car this time," Bolan said.

"Why so?" Pureza asked.

"This neighborhood isn't the best set for quick getaways. I'd feel better with you at the wheel. Less time gone to waste."

She spent a second studying his face, as if for clues to some deception, then finally nodded. "Yes. Fine."

Bolan took his Spectre SMG, muzzle-heavy with the suppressor, and moved along the dark alley, counting doors as he passed until he'd reached the rear entrance of *La Voz de la Verdad*. A motorcycle sat outside, as if to mark the place for him. The door was decorated with a small sign reading *Privado!*

Bolan tried the knob, gently, and was surprised to feel it turn in his hand. He eased the door open a crack, heard muffled voices from within and smelled the sharp tang of fresh paint.

It was a time for cautious haste, a concept that seemed con-
tradictory but which was frequently applied on battlefields. A
warrior needed to hurry sometimes, but without the all-out frenzy
of a crazy kamikaze charge.

Sometimes—and this was one of those times.

Bolan shouldered past the door, relieved to find that it had
well-oiled hinges, nostrils wrinkling as the reek of paint grew
stronger. A fluorescent light above his head showed Bolan that
the AUC members in residence were redecorating some kind of
storeroom, giving the walls a fresh coat after years of neglect.
Their brushes had been cleaned and placed to one side, as if they
were through for the day.

Beyond the next doorway, some kind of quiet party was in
progress. Three or four men were talking, laughing, but not rau-
cously. They weren't drunk yet, though he heard bottles clinking
as they toasted some remark that one had made.

He joined them, crashing the party with a simple step across
the threshold that revealed him to the four men lounging in a
kind of nonformation—two seated on metal folding chairs, one
on a stack of cardboard boxes and the last one yoga-style, on the
floor. Two rifles stood in one corner, a shotgun in another.

"Hola," Bolan said, and took them down as they reached for
their weapons, short bursts, fired at point blank range, tracking
from left to right around the room. His targets definitely knew
what hit them, but they likely had no indication as to *who*.

An oversight which he meant to correct.

Bolan returned to the first room he'd entered, grabbed a clean
paintbrush and went to work.

CRISTIANO GUZMAN'S EYES were blurred from lack of sleep.
He was exhausted, but adrenaline produced by fear denied him
any hope of sleep, even if there had been time for him to relax.
He'd broken precedent that morning, arriving an hour ahead of
his secretary and startling her by preparing the day's first pot
of coffee. When she'd asked if anything was wrong, Guzman
had forced a smile and told her that a confidential difficulty had
arisen and required his personal attention.

There was no need to suggest that he might die before the sun set.

Thus far, his efforts to locate Arcelia Pureza and identify her male companion from the north had been futile. He had grilled the lieutenant's friends and coworkers at CNP headquarters, and would happily have sent out officers to pluck her civilian informants from the streets if her notes on interviews had not been coded to conceal identities. Guzman personally had gone through the woman's desk, to no avail.

It satisfied him in an abstract sense to know that El Padrino's troops had done no better. It appeared Macario had tried to trap Pureza and her friend at Martyrs' Park, but the result had been more martyrs for the drug cartel. Guzman was not concerned about their loss—they were the scum of Bogotá—but it required no crystal ball to know that the defeat would only amplify Macario's explosive rage.

Guzman might be the next in line to feel his wrath.

And he was running out of time.

The phone purred at his elbow, a light winking to indicate his secretary's line in use. Guzman snared the receiver on the second ring.

"Yes, Anna. What is it?"

"A call from Captain Jimenez, sir. He says it's very urgent."

Guzman scowled. The call had better be damned urgent, he decided, or the captain would bitterly regret disturbing him. Instead of barking at his secretary, though, he said, "Thank you. Put him through, please."

A click in Guzman's ear, and he was saying, "Captain Jimenez, how may I assist you?"

"Sir, we have another shooting."

"Ah." Guzman could feel his stomach twisting painfully. "And are there casualties?"

"Yes, sir. Four dead."

Four men dead. Hardly impressive, after the battle at Martyrs' Park.

"Where did this happen?" Guzman asked.

"At the office of *La Voz de la Verdad*," Jimenez said.

"That weekly rag the AUC puts out?"

"Correct, sir. And this time…ah…the killers left a message."

"What kind of message?" Guzman asked, frowning.

"Painted on the wall," Captain Jimenez said. "In blood."

"Good God!" Guzman braced himself, then asked, "What does it say?"

Jimenez told him, and the deputy vice-minister's pulse kicked into overdrive. The warning throb of an impending headache flared behind his eyes.

"All right," he told Jimenez. "Take the normal photographs, then cover it. On no account must any reporters see the message or be informed of its content. Understand me, Captain?"

"Yes, sir! I understand you!"

"Any officer who leaks this information to the press can tell his pension goodbye and count on spending time in La Modelo."

"Yes, sir."

"That's all. Rush the report to me."

Guzman hung up without another word. The threat of incarceration in La Modelo—Bogotá's overcrowded and ultraviolent "model" prison—might restrain his officers from leaking information to the press, but only for a little while. The risk of being caught, in fact, was minuscule, while the rewards could be impressive.

And there'd be no keeping the story from El Padrino, of course. Guzman supposed that sooner was better than later for sharing the news. More to the point, Guzman would have to tell the tale himself, in search of a positive spin.

Fumbling in a pocket for his cell phone, he hoped that it was not already too late.

12

Pirro Aznar's headquarters was located in the small mountain municipality of El Paraíso. It hardly qualified as a town per se, being sparsely settled and with dwellings widely scattered. Local government had only been established during 1991, and the eleven councillors in charge rarely strayed outside the district's hub city at Alto de La Cruz.

Aznar enjoyed the isolation, which allowed him to be warned if enemies approached. His craving for security was not a simple fancy, but a grim prerequisite of survival as head of the Autodefensas Unidas de Colombia. Branded a terrorist by the United States and its lapdogs in Bogotá, Aznar knew he was living every day on borrowed time.

And making every minute count.

Of late, the trouble with Macario had been distracting Aznar from his central mission: the eradication from Colombia of leftists, radicals and those who scoffed at law. His stance might seem ironic—even hypocritical—to some observers, since his soldiers broke the law each time they pulled a trigger and they deigned to guard drug shipments in return for cash, but Aznar saw no inconsistency.

His was a revolutionary movement to reclaim society from those who had corrupted it. The forces presently in charge would not surrender peaceably, thus violence was required to root them out. Aznar, in his own mind, was on a par with Simón Bolivar and José de San Martín, the heroes who had liberated much of South America from foreign rule.

As for defending the Macario cartel, a revolution ran on cash, as much as patriotic dedication. When the time came, and the victory was his, Aznar would finish cleaning up his homeland and eliminate the cartel leeches. In the meantime, people like Macario made work for rural peasants, sold most of their poison in the United States, and thus helped weaken America's grip on what her leaders insultingly called the Third World.

Unfortunately, his alliance with Macario had proved costly in the past few hours. More than a dozen of Aznar's soldiers were dead, cut down in pursuit of a rogue policewoman and a man whom El Padrino could not identify, much less locate. So much vitality wasted. Such discouragement sewn among those who survived.

And as if that was not bad enough, then came the attack upon *La Voz de la Verdad* in Bogotá. A soldier sent to fetch some take-out food had come back from his errand to find CNP detectives in the office, ambulances standing by to cart the dead away. The soldier hadn't dared to ask for details, but had called Aznar as soon as he had finished counting sheeted stretchers and confirmed that his four companions were dead.

Was this another raid by the two people Macario sought?

A buzzing sound from the satellite phone distracted Aznar. He lifted the handset, adopting a world-weary tone as he answered.

"Hello."

"Pirro Aznar?" a strange voice asked.

"Who are you?" Aznar said.

"Just a messenger," the deep male voice said. "Has anybody tipped you off about your newspaper?"

"I am informed of the events."

"Including what the cops found on the wall?" his caller asked.

The question drew a worry line between Aznar's eyebrows. "I am not sure what you refer to."

"So, they've got it under wraps. I'm not surprised. They're likely worried what would happen if you knew."

"Knew what?"

"About the writing. Done in blood."

"Blood?"

"I suppose your people didn't need it anymore," the stranger said.

"You say there was a message?"

"I suppose that's pushing it. A name is what I heard. But maybe there's a message in it for you."

"*What* name?"

"El Padrino. That make any sense to you?" The silence stretched between them for a moment, Aznar at a loss for words, until the caller said, "I guess it does."

And broke the link.

"Señor? Señor!"

Dead air.

Thinking swiftly, Aznar dialed a number and waited, grinding his teeth through four rings until the distant telephone was answered.

"Camilo! I need you to check on *La Voz*... Yes, I know they were killed... Yes. Be quiet and listen! I need to know if anything was written on the walls... That's what I said... Call our friend at *El Espectador* and see if he's heard anything... Call anyone you can think of who might know the answer... When? This second!"

His turn to cut the link and leave someone fuming, content in the knowledge that Camilo would track down the information required to confirm or refute the anonymous caller's report.

And if it proved true, what should Aznar make of the blood graffiti? Was it meant to blame him for supporting El Padrino, or had Macario himself sent the message? If so, for what purpose?

In any case, Aznar already knew one thing.

He should prepare for all-out war.

Rolling past the University City of Bogotá, locally known as *Ciudad Blanca* for its tall white buildings, Bolan closed his cell phone and said, "That ought to stir the pot."

"You think he will turn on Macario?" Pureza asked.

"He'll start to think about it, anyway," Bolan replied. "Another push or two and he won't have much choice."

"What if Macario tries to explain?"

"I'm counting on it," Bolan said. "With any luck, the more he talks, the more suspicious Aznar will be."

"You're very devious," she said, smiling.

"Just doing what I can with what I've got."

"And where is our next push to be delivered?"

"Someplace that will hurt the AUC," he said. "Stir up the hornet's nest."

Pureza thought about it for a moment, then replied, "You've silenced one of the movement's voices. Why not another?"

"What would that be?" Bolan asked.

"They have a broadcast station near the university," she said. "For radio. From Bogotá its range covers Cundinamarca, parts of Meta and Tolima."

"And it's legal?" Bolan asked.

"Of course. Our laws ensure freedom of speech and the press, as do yours, except in cases of terrorist threats and incitements to violence. The AUC is generally careful not to cross that line with any public statement, though it calls for sweeping change and fails to specify the means."

"So, if we pull the plug…"

"Aznar will feel it. Certainly."

"And if he thinks Macario's responsible—"

"Then we divide and conquer, yes?"

"Sounds like a plan."

She pointed Bolan toward the station, situated in a bungalow behind a shabby-looking thrift shop also operated by the AUC. Scanning the place, Bolan adjusted his intentions to include the store. Two birds, one stone.

A motorcycle and an old Honda sedan were parked outside the radio station, with no sign of any guards patrolling the grounds.

Bolan parked the Pontiac a half block to the west and walked back with Pureza at his side, eyes sweeping the landscape for any sign of a trap, finding none.

All clear...and yet, it still felt *wrong*.

"Wait here," he whispered, steering Pureza into cover behind a fenced pen that contained two old garbage Dumpsters. Bolan went on alone, approaching the bungalow's rear in broad daylight, one hand on the grip of his silenced Spectre SMG.

One of the back windows was open and he stood beneath it, eavesdropping. Though the conversation was too muffled to pick out what they were saying, his ears picked out four distinct voices.

And how many others not talking?

One way to find out.

Bolan took a frag grenade from his pocket, clutching it in his left hand and pulled the safety pin. His right hand raised the Spectre, triggered a short burst that shredded the window screen, mangling the ceiling inside, then he followed up with the grenade and high-stepped toward the nearest corner for cover.

The blast, contained, wasn't as loud as Hollywood FX teams always made it seem. The other windows shattered, spewing smoky dust, but no great ball of fire erupted to consume the bungalow. The killing impact of a frag grenade lay in its shrapnel, not in any blazing conflagration.

Bolan ran around to the front door, Pureza trailing, and arrived just as a member of the AUC lurched into view, trying to clear the blood out of his eyes with his sleeve. Bolan squeezed off a 3-round burst that ended all of the guerrilla's worries on the spot, then stepped across his body, lunging through the open doorway.

The other three were down and out, at least for the moment. He didn't check for pulses, left fate to decide if they would live or die. Scouting the place, he found a cupboard filled with useful items that included several cans of spray paint, maybe used for some promotional activity. Bolan chose red, stepped back outside and left his tag.

"The store, next?" Pureza asked.

"The store," Bolan confirmed, turning in that direction as he freed a thermite canister from its belt clip.

NALDO MACARIO HAD LEARNED to hate the telephone. It brought only bad news these days, and if he heard one more report of a defeat by the woman and gringo who had turned his world upside down within half a day, Macario thought that he might run amok.

Still, he answered when the phone rang, since it was his private line. Perhaps, he thought, Quintaro might be calling to explain why he had disappeared after the fight at Martyrs' Park. Or perhaps it was Santiago Villegas, eager to report that he had found the lieutenant and her cohort. That the two of them were cornered, trapped—or better yet, stone-dead.

But no.

He recognized Cristiano Guzman's voice as soon as the bureaucrat said, "Mr. Macario?"

"Who else ever answers this line?"

"Of course! I apologize, sir."

"Have you simply called me to apologize?" Macario inquired.

"No, no. I have new information...but I fear it may disturb you."

"Just speak!"

Guzman described the raid upon the office of *La Voz de la Verdad,* with four of Aznar's AUC guerrillas killed. Macario had no great interest in their welfare, and was just about to say so when the deputy vice-minister added, "There was a message at the murder scene, *señor.* Painted in blood."

"What? Blood?"

"Yes, sir. On the wall, I'm told."

Well, strange things happened in the world of Latin revolutionary politics. Macario himself had scrawled a note or two in blood when he was younger, fighting his way up the food chain from Bogotá's gutter to the pinnacle of wealth and power.

"May I assume there is some relevance?" Dreading the answer even as he spoke, Macario asked, "What did this message say?"

"El Padrino."

"Yes, I'm waiting."

"No, sir. That's what was written on the wall," Guzman explained. "The killers painted 'El Padrino.'"

Macario let that soak in, then said, "They signed my name."

"Yes, sir. I have taken steps to keep it from the media, of course, but with so many officers involved, bystanders on the street and so on, it is bound to be exposed."

"Thank you," Macario replied. "Keep me informed of any new developments."

He cut the link, his mind already grappling with the puzzle. He could think of only two reasons why someone might have signed the crime scene with his name. First, one of his own men might do it without orders, in a moment of excitement, if he was drunk or high on cocaine. In which case, Macario would personally flay the imbecile alive, making it last for days and marching all his other soldiers through the butcher shop as an indelible object lesson.

Or second, an enemy might have signed his name to the murders in an effort to embarrass Macario in the media, cause police to suspect him of the crime...or to create a rift between himself and the AUC.

Of course! It was so obvious a child could work it out.

But what about Pirro Aznar?

The AUC's commanding officer considered himself a deep political thinker, but in truth his philosophy was mostly lifted from pamphlets published by other far-right groups that had gone before him, trumpeting nationalism, free enterprise, and rigid law enforcement that was honored more in the breach than the observance. Stripped of others' rhetoric, Aznar was a brutish street fighter, a mediocre tactician and no great intellect at all.

Would he fall for the ruse? Very possibly, unless Macario could talk him out of it.

Assuming that the news had reached Aznar's ears already, Macario took a moment to frame his thoughts, rehearsing his words for maximum effect. He could not ramble or allow himself to be distracted. And above all else, he had to deal with Aznar from strength, with no hint of a groveling apology for something that his enemies had done.

Translating thought into action, Macario dialed Aznar's unlisted number, paced through four long rings, then heard an unfamiliar voice say, "What?"

Macario identified himself and told the flunky to put Aznar on the line, wasting no time on common courtesy with underlings. A full minute passed before he picked up and started speaking rapidly, drowning Macario in angry words.

"You have the nerve to call me, after what you've done? Bastard! If you want a war, you'll have one!"

"Pirro, wait!" Macario despised the weak, defensive tone of his own voice. "You've been deceived. I did not do this thing."

"Which thing, exactly?" Aznar challenged him.

"*La Voz de la Verdad*," Macario replied, feeling confusion wriggle in his head. "My men did not attack the office. Why would they?"

"I don't know, Padrino," Aznar spit, twisting Macario's honorific title into a mocking slur. "Perhaps for the same reason that they destroyed our radio station and its thrift shop?"

Macario felt as if he were losing his mind. *What* radio station? *What* thrift shop? "I don't know what you're talking about," he replied. "There has been some mistake."

"And you made it," Aznar said.

Just before the line went dead.

"So, DO WE TAG THE NEXT place with an 'AUC,'" Pureza asked, as the Pontiac G6 rolled through the neighborhood known as San Vicente Ferrer, en route toward their next chosen target.

"Too obvious," Bolan replied. "If Macario and Aznar start comparing notes it could cost us the game. We'll leave Macario guessing who did it this time."

Still wondering what made this soldier tick, as the Americans would say, she asked, "Who taught you all of this?"

He hesitated, as if considering how much to share, then said,

"The army got me started as a kid through Special Forces. Then I picked the rest up as I went along."

"Fighting the drug dealers?"

"Among others," Bolan said.

"Your life must be…unusual."

"You're in the middle of it," he reminded her. "So you tell me."

"It's frightening," Pureza said. "But also…liberating, I believe you say."

"I never really thought of it that way."

"To break the rules and do what must be done against the scum like El Padrino, yet to know that you are on the angels' side."

That put a frown on Bolan's face. "You'd have a hard time selling that to any clergyman in town," he said.

"Perhaps because they've turned their backs on justice and the faith required to seek it."

"That's too deep for me," Bolan replied. "I'm just a soldier with a mission, trying not to blow it."

"You're too modest," Pureza said.

"A big head makes a tempting target," Bolan said, then, "Here we are."

The target was a warehouse that Macario had converted into a sound stage for production of pornographic films. The Colombian Institute for Family Welfare estimated that thirty thousand children were forced into commercial sex work every year, and while no charges had been filed against Macario or anyone from his cartel, Pureza already had one side of the ugly business tonight.

And here was another.

The place revealed no sign of life as Bolan drove around the block, examining it from the front and rear. Its parking lot was empty, and its garbage Dumpster, too, from what Pureza could see in passing.

"I suspect we missed the party," Bolan said.

"Perhaps Macario cannot defend all of his property at once," Pureza suggested.

"Good for us, and bad for him," Bolan replied.

He boldly turned into the warehouse parking lot, made a U-turn and backed up to the loading dock. From there, Pureza could see a padlock on the nearest door.

"You're right," she said. "They've gone from here."

"No problem," Bolan said. "I'll just leave a housewarming gift, and we'll be on our way."

She recognized the incendiary grenade when he removed it from the duffel bag behind his seat. "I'll scout around in back," he said. "Make sure the other doors are locked up tight and no one's home. Wait here."

Pureza watched him disappear around the southwest corner of the warehouse, then turned her attention to the street before her. Traffic flowed as if it was another ordinary day in Bogotá—which, she supposed, it was for those who passed the warehouse on their way to jobs, schools, love affairs and other trifling business of the human herd.

How strange it was to realize that even as she fought on their behalf, risking her life, the sheep went on about their mundane tasks, unaware of the war that raged around them, mostly out of sight and out of mind.

Bolan returned two minutes later, slid into the driver's seat and said, "It's set. We're out of here."

There was no sign of smoke before they reached the street and merged with traffic, but Pureza imagined the grenade's explosion, spewing white-hot coals, filling a place of shame with smoke and fire. How many billion pesos would it cost Macario?

Not nearly enough.

"Who next?" she asked. "The cartel or the AUC?"

"Let's make it AUC," he said. "I'm trying to be fair."

13

Usaquén District, Bogotá

Macario had not felt anything approaching panic since the age of twelve, when he had knifed his first victim to death in the Ciudad Bolívar slums. Afterward in that case, it had been a fear of capture and imprisonment or worse, which quickly faded as he realized that no one cared about one more child of the street sent to God.

On this day his worry, or fear—though not yet panic, but drifting in that grim direction—involved powerful men who *would* care if he failed them because he could not control one or two enemies bent on disrupting his trade. Those men, potential business partners, were arriving on this very day in Bogotá, to discuss a broader, vastly more profitable alliance with Macario's cartel.

And what would they think if they found him besieged? How would these wealthy, ruthless men from the United States, Europe and Asia look upon a man who couldn't stop two people—one of them a woman—from killing his soldiers, costing him millions, spitting in his face with impunity?

At best, they would dismiss him as an overrated amateur, decline his offers of partnership and perhaps go shopping for a new cocaine supplier. The Hidalgo brothers in Barranquilla perhaps, or Andrés Gamboa in Popayán. At worst, the outsiders might see Macario's territory as a plum ripe for picking and plot to move in themselves, take control behind hired local fronts while the bulk of the profits flew north, east, or west.

Macario was not about to let that happen. First, while he could not prevent his guests from learning of the troubles he had suffered—most or all of them would know the basic facts before their planes touched down in Bogotá—he would pull every string at his command to keep the recent violence from touching them in any way.

Second, he would do everything within his power to prevent the several foreign delegations from collaborating to his detriment. Some were rivals already, while others were allies. In a bid to isolate them slightly, Macario had booked each delegation into a different five-star hotel—Americans at the Tequendama Inter-Continental, Japanese at the Lugano Imperial Suites, Sicilians at the Charleston, Russians at the Palacio Domain and Chinese at the Casa Medina.

Third, while some of Macario's plans for entertaining his guests had gone up in smoke, he thought he could still keep them reasonably happy with the best food available in Bogotá and a stable of willing Colombian beauties. One of the Russians, he had learned, also enjoyed boys, a taste that Macario personally despised but which he could accommodate despite the recent fiery outing of his most expensive pedo-brothel.

Anything was available in Bogotá, for a price.

The bad news was that security risks for the meeting had doubled, with Macario facing the prospect of a feud with the AUC in addition to his other, seemingly insoluble problem. At any other time he would have simply killed Pirro Aznar, but if a shooting war could be avoided for the next few days at least, Macario stood to profit hugely from the stall.

To that end, he'd recalled his new lieutenant from the hunt for Arcelia Pureza and her unknown gringo companion, tasking him instead to double-check and triple-check security around the five hotels where Macario's guests would be spending the weekend. Five stretch limousines, all armored, were on standby with armed guards and drivers trained in evasive techniques.

Macario had also spoken urgently to Cristiano Guzman, receiving the deputy vice-minister's personal assurance that no police or military personnel would even dream of interfering with his visitors. Guzman, he knew, had spoken truthfully on that account.

Because his very life depended on it.

In a nation where no one was safe anytime, anywhere, Guzman had to realize that failure in this task meant more than simply being cut off from the flow of bribes that let him live light-years beyond his means. It meant, at best, a sudden bloody death—perhaps for everyone Guzman held dear.

And even if he truly loved no one except himself, that would be threat enough.

Craving a drink, Macario poured himself a double shot of *aguardiente* and gulped it down in one swallow. The heat struck him first, as always, then a tingling in his fingertips and at his nape. It was unwise, he had been told to drink as a relief from stress, but when was liquor needed more? Or any other drug?

If all the world did what was wise, healthy and safe, Macario would never earn another peso in his life. Thank Chango, Oshún and the other gods of Santeria, there appeared to be no risk of that.

Ciudad Bolívar District, Bogotá

"WHAT GALL HE HAS!" Aznar snarled. "That piece of crap thinks I'm a fool. He thinks that a phone call will make me forget what he's done."

"Perhaps…" Léon Rivera stopped, leaving the thought unfinished, unexpressed.

"What?" Aznar demanded of his second in command. "Speak up!"

"Perhaps," Rivera said, "Macario is not responsible for the attacks."

"Are you crazy?" Aznar asked.

"No, sir. I ask myself why El Padrino would turn on us at a time when he needs our support most. That seems loco to me. Then to call you as if he's done nothing?"

"It's part of his plan," Aznar said, unconvinced. "He wants to start me questioning my senses, don't you see? Make me believe that the attacks were executed by this woman and her gringo friend Macario keeps hunting high and low."

"And if they were?" Rivera asked.

"Impossible," Aznar said. "Those two want Macario and his men, not the AUC."

Rivera shrugged, still looking unconvinced.

"You disagree, Léon?"

"We know that the Americans despise us," Rivera said. "Their State Department calls us narcoterrorists, as if we are any different from the Contras they supported in Nicaragua. Why would their man not attack us while he is pursuing Macario?"

Aznar considered it, saw that there was a certain logic to Rivera's words, but still his rage against Macario would not subside.

"You know it's not unusual for El Padrino—" Aznar fairly spat the name "—to sign his handiwork. We've seen these kinds of messages before. He does it to impress his enemies without giving police enough to hang him."

"And the CIA would know that, yes? The DEA? The FBI?" Rivera asked.

"You make a point," Aznar acknowledged. "But if what you say is true, why wouldn't he explain as much to me?"

"Perhaps he tried," Rivera said. "You *did* hang up on him, sir."

"And what do you suggest, Léon? That I should call him back and apologize? Beg El Padrino's forgiveness?"

"No one mentioned begging, Pirro. But to speak with him… what could it hurt?"

The taste of bitter gall made Aznar grimace. Few things made him more upset than being wrong, and while he wasn't ready to admit that Rivera was correct, he owed it to himself—and to his soldiers who would die in any struggle with Macario—to be damned sure that he was right before he charged ahead.

"Okay," he said at last, reluctantly. "I'll call, as you suggest."

He had Macario's safe line on speed dial. Seconds later, Aznar stood with Rivera, watching him, and listened to the distant ringing of a telephone at El Padrino's home. An unfamiliar voice responded on the fourth ring.

"Who is it?"

Aznar gave his name, asked for Macario. The stranger on the other end responded instantly, "You are dead to El Padrino. You had better go hide and pray."

And then the line went dead.

"Pirro? What is it?" Rivera asked.

Aznar's voice was stiff with fury as he answered. "One of Naldo's men. He says I'm dead to them. He says that I should find a place to hide and pray."

"Pirro—"

"That son of a bitch tells a flunky to say this? To *me?*" Aznar raged.

"You were right, Pirro. He has betrayed us."

"And he will pay for this treachery. I swear it on the blood of those he's murdered."

"You've said he is expecting guests," Rivera said. "Rich foreigners?"

"More criminals," Aznar replied. "Scum of the earth."

"But still important to Macario, right?"

"To help his business, yes."

"And if their time in Bogotá should disappoint them, it would hurt him."

Aznar smiled. "Or better still, if some of them did not survive. Their syndicates would take a dim view of Macario, I think."

"We know his weakness, then," Rivera said.

"And we can use it to destroy him," Aznar said.

"For the people," Rivera said.

"Yes, for the people," Aznar agreed. "And as a lesson to our enemies."

Macario had been a major source of funding for the AUC, until some madness had compelled him to betray Aznar. Motive no longer mattered. Only what Macario had done, and how his treachery might be repaid in kind.

The good news: after serving the cartel for cash, Aznar could strike a blow against the drug trafficking leeches who polluted Colombian society from top to bottom. In the process, he might even make himself a hero.

At the very least, he would enjoy the taste of sweet revenge.

Rafael Uribe District, Bogotá

"WE NEED A PAIR OF EYES inside," Bolan said as they motored through the neighborhood of Las Colinas, passing from one target to the next. Behind them lay another burning warehouse, used by El Padrino to store contraband in transit. Ahead lay...who could say?

Pureza frowned. "And by 'inside' you mean...?"

"Inside Macario's cartel," Bolan replied. "I can't call up and ask him how he's feeling, what he plans for his next move. But someone who's around him would be helpful."

"A lieutenant?" she suggested.

"Even further down the ladder. Say a sergeant, or a corporal who keeps his eyes peeled. People in a mob like that know things—whether the boss wants them to or not."

"Where do we start?" she asked—the *we* no longer sounded strange to her ears.

"Not headquarters," he said. "Someplace we'll have a reasonable chance of finding what we need without a major firefight."

"Club El Dorado," she replied with every confidence.

"Which is...?"

"Macario's casino. It's a few miles north of here, in Ciudad Montes."

"Open at this time of day?" Bolan asked.

"Open always, like your own Las Vegas or Atlantic City."

"Perfect," he said. "I feel a sudden urge to roll the dice."

Club El Dorado occupied a city block on Avenida Primero de Mayo, between Calle 40 and Calle 40A. It was in fact a kind of mini-Vegas operation, complete with garish neon—muted by daylight—depicting a huge roulette wheel and a five-card poker hand whose cards "flipped" to reveal a royal flush. Street-level posters under plastic advertised musical acts and dancing girls whose costumes left nothing to the imagination.

Bolan bypassed the valets in front and left the Pontiac in a parking lot around back. Pureza joined him on the muggy walk to sliding doors that opened with a frigid blast of air-conditioning that chilled her skin. Crossing the threshold, they were instantly enveloped by the smells and sounds common to every large casino in the world.

Pureza had been to the casino several times and remembered the layout. "The office is this way," she said, steering Bolan to the left, past banks of slot machines positioned to catch players coming and going, their lights flashing gaily, some warbling mechanical music.

They reached a staircase, closed to public access by a velvet rope with a dangling sign that read in Spanish: Private—Employees Only.

"I don't think they'll mind us intruding," Pureza said, unhooking one end of the rope and letting it drop.

"I like crashing parties," Bolan said.

She couldn't help smiling. "I guessed that about you."

Another Private warning marked the office door upstairs, but Bolan ignored it, breezing through with his pistol in hand. Pureza, with her own gun drawn, remained a pace behind him, addressing the room in Spanish.

"Everyone remain calm! No alarms!"

The three people present stood silent as ordered, sounding no alarms. Pureza dismissed a cocktail waitress and a croupier with a wave of her pistol, focusing on the club's manager.

"Jaime Mendez," she said.

"Do we know each other?" he asked in Spanish.

"No, we haven't met," she responded in English. "We're making amends for that now."

"I don't understand," Mendez said.

"We'll explain on the way," Bolan said. "Where's the closet?"

Mendez nodded to a nearby door that opened on a walk-in closet used to store office supplies. Pureza prodded the two employees inside, shut the door and wedged a handy chair beneath the doorknob. It would hold them long enough without putting the pair at serious risk.

"All right," she told Mendez. "Let's go."

"Where are we going?"

"Someplace we can have a little chat, uninterrupted," Bolan said.

"I can't just go," the manager insisted.

Bolan made a little waggling motion with his Glock and said, "I bet you can."

"Cause no alarm as we are leaving," Pureza said. "It would be a grave mistake."

"Yes, I understand."

For appearances, they trailed Mendez out of the office, down the stairs and toward the exit. On the way, a club employee stopped the manager to ask about a roulette player who desired to raise the table's betting limit. Mendez cleared it and moved on, flanked by his apparent guards as they left the casino.

"This way," Pureza said, guiding their captive with a light touch on his arm. She was prepared to draw her weapon if he bolted, but Mendez seemed cowed.

And by the time they reached the Pontiac, he had begun to weep. "Are you going to kill me right here?" he asked in Spanish, with a hitch in his voice.

"We don't want to kill you here," Pureza said. "Or anywhere, if you cooperate."

"But how?"

"Get in the car," Bolan advised. "With any luck, this time tomorrow you could be the one who got away."

SLUMPED AT HIS DESK WITH a scowl on his face, Cristiano Guzman recalled the old saying about being worse off than a prostitute in Holy Week. And indeed he was.

It had been bad enough when he was tasked to find the vanished Lieutenant Arcelia Pureza and her unknown American cohort. But now, Macario demanded even more—specifically, protection for a list of criminals arriving within the next hours from various parts of the world for a meeting inside Bogotá.

On this day, of all days.

He had a list of names, flight numbers and arrival times. El Padrino had spared him the humiliation of providing uniformed guards for the unsavory tourists, but Guzman still had to ensure that none of his investigators or patrolmen troubled them in any way.

Scanning the list provoked a sour feeling in his stomach, a rancid taste in his mouth.

From New York City, Fausto Ciampi and Stefano d'Arezzo. From Saint Petersburg, Russia, Anton Gergiev and Tikhon Polekh. From Kyoto, Japan, Mori Saburo and Kanata Hitoshi. From Palermo, Sicily, by way of Naples, Bruno Manzoni and Marsilio Bonino. From Hong Kong, Jiang Kemin and Liu Xian. All accompanied, of course, by aides and bodyguards.

Guzman did not require a briefing from the CNP's Police Intelligence Directorate to recognize the organizations those men represented. Macario was hosting leaders of the American Cosa Nostra, the Russian Bratva, Japan's Yakuza, the Chinese triads and Sicily's Mafia, gathered in Bogotá at the worst of all possible times.

And there was nothing Guzman could do to stop it.

How had his life and one-time promising career degenerated to its present sorry state? Guzman knew he could blame no one except himself. Colombia had law enforcement officers and politicians who were brave enough to stand against the drug cartels without accepting bribes and coddling vicious felons. Granted, some of them were dead, but others still survived and did their quiet work as best they could.

Guzman, by contrast, had surrendered to ambition and to

avarice. His job, his reputation and his life were on the line because he had been weak, greedy and foolish.

But he saw no options. He had to forge ahead and do as he was told, hope for the best and keep his passport handy, with the passbooks to his secret bank accounts, in case he had to flee the country at a moment's notice. He had considered warning his mistress, having her packed and ready when the time came, then decided excess baggage could be fatal in a pinch.

Perhaps someday she'd understand. If not, too bad.

Guzman had a suitcase ready in the trunk of his Mercedes-Benz. He also had a pistol in the glove compartment and another tucked under his belt. It spoiled the line of his expensive suit, but so would bullet holes.

It had become a waiting game, its outcome unpredictable. At this time yesterday, Guzman would have believed that El Padrino was invincible. This day it seemed like even money whether he would win or lose the battle that had cost so many lives, destroying so much property. And with the delegates from foreign syndicates arriving any minute, did it mean an end to the rebellion? Or simply more targets for bloodthirsty guns?

Since his return to the office that morning, after a futile attempt at sleep, Guzman had been shredding his sensitive files. No trace remained of his links to Macario—or, at least, not within the Palace of Justice. By the time Macario considered using any evidence of involvement against Guzman, the deputy vice-minister could be across the border and well out of reach, winging his way to freedom and a better life under a new identity.

But not just yet.

He needed to remain and judge the final state of play in Bogotá, see for himself if flight was necessary, or if El Padrino's world would crumble, burying Macario and leaving Guzman free to pick up with his life where it had been disrupted....

He waited, watched the clock and offered up a silent prayer that something might be salvaged from the ruin of his life.

14

Jaime Mendez had spilled his guts without the need of spilling any blood. His tough talk had evaporated on the ride to one of Pureza's scattered safehouses, and once presented with a final choice of life or death the casino manager had given up the knowledge he possessed without a fight.

Next Bolan simply had to make some sense of it.

Because their hostage was primarily involved with the casino's operation, rather than the larger strategy of daily cartel action in the field, his view was limited. Still, he'd been told that several important foreigners were coming into Bogotá over the weekend. If they chose to visit the casino, El Padrino was prepared to comp them each a million pesos for play on the house.

As to who these guests were, Mendez couldn't say. He *did* know that they were coming in pairs, two from the United States, two from Italy, two from somewhere in Russia, two from Japan and two more from China. After hearing that, the names became superfluous to Bolan.

"It's a sit-down," he advised Pureza. "Must be. Macario's got buyers coming in from all over the world. Smart money says they represent the leading syndicates in their home territories."

"Russian *mafiya?*" she asked.

He nodded. "And the U.S. version, plus the triads and the Yakuza. On the two Italians, you could flip a coin. If their trip starts in Sicily, they're Mafia. If not, they could be Camorra, 'Ndrangheta or Sacra Corona Unita. Names change, but they all smell the same."

"Macario will be concerned with their security and with the progress of negotiations," Pureza said.

"He must be going nuts," Bolan agreed. "Afraid that we might crash the party."

"And shall we?"

Bolan smiled. "I wouldn't miss it for the world. But first, I need to pick up something special."

"Which would be…?"

"Something I saw when I was shopping for my other tools. Let's call it a housewarming gift."

"It's impolite to tease," she warned him.

"Patience," Bolan counseled. "First we have to deal with Jaime here."

"What will you do with him?" Pureza asked.

"He's part of the Macario machine," Bolan replied. "The world's most likely better off without him."

"He only runs a gambling club," Pureza answered.

"That we know of."

"And we promised him his life if he cooperated."

"Yes, we did," Bolan said. "But we need to keep him out of circulation while we finish up this thing. Macario most likely knows we have him, from the visual descriptions, but let's keep him guessing on the intel."

"Leave him here?" Pureza suggested.

"He'd have to be secured."

"There are shackles here."

"Okay. We'd have to keep him quiet, too."

"A gag. There also may be sedatives. I'll have to check the bathroom."

"Okay, then. Let's wrap him up and hit the road. One thing, though."

"What?"

"In case we don't come back or aren't in any shape to make a call…"

She frowned and nodded. "We can chain him in the bathroom, eh? I'll leave the tap running for water, and he'll have the toilet. Cuff his hands behind his back, so he cannot unfasten any of the bolts or pipes."

"Good thinking. Have you done this kind of thing before?"

Pureza smiled. "There is a first time, as they say, for everything."

SANTIAGO VILLEGAS double-checked his watch against a large clock mounted on the north wall of the international arrivals and departures terminal inside the El Dorado International Airport. The two-minute discrepancy was insignificant. What mattered was a flashing message that informed him that the Japan Airlines flight from Kyoto had landed on time.

Villegas waited with two of Macario's men at the point where their guests from Japan should emerge any moment. Security procedures barred him from the actual arrival gate, but he could still escort them to the baggage carousels and on from there to El Padrino's waiting limousine.

And if that wasn't good enough, to hell with them.

Villegas would say no such thing, of course, or even give them cause to think his mind might harbor any thoughts of insubordination. El Padrino's orders were explicit: Villegas was to retrieve the Japanese and guarantee their comfort—not to mention safety—on the ride to their hotel. Once they had settled in, another team would fetch them and take them to his estate.

And there they were. Two Japanese men of middle age, flanked by a pair of younger men who had to be bodyguards. Villegas had been shown their photographs and drilled on the pronunciation of their names, ordered to greet the older of them first.

"Good day," he said through a tight plastic smile, remembering to bow a bit instead of offering his hand. "Mr. Mori. Mr. Kanata. Welcome to Bogotá. I am Santiago Villegas, sent by Mr. Macario to meet and transport you to your hotel."

The man Villegas knew as Mori Saburo said, "He did not come himself."

It wasn't a question, but it clearly demanded an answer. Villegas saw the trap yawning before him.

"No, sir." Improvising, he added, "Mr. Macario felt that with so many honored guests arriving on this day, he should supervise all aspects of your comfort and accommodation."

"Hmpf," was the man's only response.

They proceeded toward the baggage area and waited to retrieve the party's luggage, found a porter with a cart to haul it and then left the terminal to find the limousine. It was a twenty-minute ride to their hotel, the lavish Lugano Imperial Suites, on Calle 70 north of Avenida de las Americas.

The new arrivals asked no questions while in transit, which suited Villegas perfectly. He was content to march them through the hotel's lobby to the registration desk, and to remind the manager that El Padrino would be picking up the tab. All smiles, the manager assured Villegas that the travelers were in good hands.

Checking his watch again, Villegas saw that it was time to make his next stop at the airport. Number two of four, since two parties—American and Russian—were arriving within moments of each other. He would greet them both, load one into a second limousine already waiting at the terminal, and thus continue with his duties as a concierge and taxi driver.

But Villegas wished that he was hunting for his boss's enemies. He could not shake the feeling that they would return to haunt him soon, and that he would regret the time wasted on pleasantries with strangers.

Still, if they were drawn to foreign bait, he might yet have a chance to kill them both. The prospect put a smile on Villegas' face.

"SO, THIS IS IT?" PUREZA asked, as Bolan parked outside the pawn shop on Calle Primero de Mayo.

"It doesn't look like much, I grant you," he replied. "But wait until you see the inventory."

"I can hardly wait," she answered, sounding skeptical.

The shop's proprietor remembered Bolan, beaming as he crossed the floor to greet him, nodding at Pureza.

"You wish more special merchandise, *señor?*"

"Something I saw last time but lacked the foresight to acquire," Bolan replied.

"Of course! Please, come with me."

After he locked the shop's front door and switched its sign to read *Cerrado,* he led Bolan and Pureza to his secret armory. Bolan watched the police lieutenant's eyes widen at first glimpse of the racked and ready weapons.

"There it is," Bolan said, veering toward the arsenal's east wall.

The weapon was a Hawk MM-1 semiautomatic grenade launcher. It resembled an old-fashioned Tommy gun on steroids, with the shoulder stock removed, its heavy spring-loaded cylinder accommodating twelve 40 mm rounds. It measured twenty-five inches from pistol grip to muzzle and weighed close to thirteen pounds unloaded. The manufacturer claimed point accuracy at 150 yards and area accuracy for explosive rounds at 350 yards.

Bolan had used the MM-1 before and liked it. Setting the launcher aside, he browsed the available ammo supply, choosing a hundred rounds each of buckshot, high explosive and incendiary in 25-round bandoliers.

"So many?" Pureza asked.

"I'd rather have them and not need them—"

"Than need them and not have them, *sí.*"

"A wise decision," the merchant said, ringing up the pesos in his head. "And if there is anything else…?"

"That should do it," Bolan said.

"Of course, as you say." The dealer quoted a price, watched Bolan lay out the bills, nodding in satisfaction as he hit the asking price. "*Muy bueno, señor.* Always a pleasure."

"No doubt," Bolan said, as he loaded his new purchases into three duffel bags. Pureza took the MM-1, leaving Bolan the two bags of grenades, close to eighty pounds each. Leaving the shop, he thought they looked like any other couple carting unexpected bargains to their car.

As for the dealer, Bolan guessed he didn't know or care that items sold that morning might be used to kill off other paying customers that afternoon. It was the nature of the business. Life went on.

For some.

FAUSTO CIAMPI'S MOOD had soured on the long flight south from JFK to Bogotá. He'd seen the in-flight movie twice before, the so-called "first-class" meal he had reminded him of something from a lousy fast-food joint and worrying about the meet that lay ahead had kept him from sleeping.

Bogotá was dangerous. He'd known that going in, but still agreed to meet Naldo Macario on his home turf because the goddamned Feds were snapping at Ciampi's heels around the clock, making his life a misery. He needed new product to peddle on the street, new partners and new opportunities if he was going to revive his failing Family and hold on to the power that its name once wielded in New York.

There'd been a time... But hell, he couldn't dwell on that. He could rave about the good old days until the friggin' cows came home, and still accomplish absolutely squat. If there was no relief forthcoming from Colombia, he'd have to put out feelers to the Mexicans, maybe the damned Jamaicans, and he hated doing that.

As they were circling into their approach, Ciampi turned to his adviser in the window seat and said, "We need to watch this guy. And I mean watch him like a fuckin' hawk."

"We'll watch him," Stefano d'Arezzo replied.

"No funny stuff to get us waxed down here, you know," Ciampi said, "but if you smell a rat, give me a signal, eh? Then we can go through all the motions, get our asses home and blow him off."

"He won't like that," d'Arezzo said.

"Fuck a bunch of what he doesn't like," Ciampi growled. "He wants to come up in the boroughs and start somethin', then we'll see who goes home in a box."

Their plane touched down, sending a nervous jolt through

Ciampi's bowels, but he fought it and kept his face blank. The best thing about first-class traveling these days was being first to leave the plane and clear the Jetway, breathing the recycled air that smelled the same in every airport he had ever used.

They moved along the concourse, flanked by two young soldiers, following bilingual signs that told them where to go. Beyond security, where lines of people waited to be searched before boarding, Ciampi saw a cluster of tough-looking people away to his left.

"Watch these guys," he told the bodyguards, as the welcoming committee surged forward to greet them.

One of the locals offered a long-fingered hand and said, "Welcome to Bogotá Señor Ciampi, Señor d'Arezzo. I am Santiago Villegas."

"The tour guide, I take it?" Ciampi asked.

"As you say, *señor*. We have a second delegation landing any moment, from Saint Petersburg, but I hope to have you on your way by then to your hotel."

"I hope it's halfway decent," Ciampi said.

"More than half, *señor*. The Tequendama InterContinental is outstanding, known for lavish service and superior accommodations."

"Guess we'll see. You gonna help us get our bags before you stick us on the shuttle bus?"

"No bus, *señor*," their guide said, feigning horror. "El Padrino has a limousine awaiting you, as soon as we retrieve your luggage."

"May as well get to it then," Ciampi said. And turning, he whispered to d'Arezzo, "El Padrino, shit. He ain't my friggin' godfather."

Hotel Casa Medina, Bogotá

JIANG KEMIN WAS SATISFIED with his hotel suite, but it suffered by comparison with his penthouse apartment in Hong Kong. Leaving his bodyguard to unpack his suitcases, he went next door to Liu Xian's suite, knocked softly and was instantly admitted to another room resembling his own in all particulars, except for choice of artwork on the walls.

So much for Western individuality.

"Sir," his lieutenant said, "are your accommodations satisfactory?"

"They are apparently identical to yours," Jiang replied.

"I can demand improvement of your quarters if—"

Jiang raised a hand to silence him. "There is no need. I can endure the local form of 'luxury' for one weekend."

"Of course."

"How long before the car returns and takes us to our host?" Jiang knew the answer, but it was required of an important man to seem detached, even distracted.

"Two more hours," Liu said, playing the game.

"What are your first impressions of our hosts?"

"The emissary had been taught to bow instead of shaking hands. That indicates at least a superficial effort to be courteous. I still advise the utmost caution dealing with these people. They are little more than gross barbarians."

"Agreed. But *useful* gross barbarians, perhaps," Jiang replied.

"Of course. Exactly as you say."

Jiang Kemin was mountain master of the 14K Triad, its ultimate commander. Liu Xian served as his vanguard, a kind of administrative officer and adviser on par with the consigliere of a Mafia Family. Jiang alone would decide whether his syndicate forged an alliance with Macario, but he trusted Liu to examine the deal with fresh eyes and report what he saw.

As for security, their bodyguards were two of Hong Kong's toughest and most feared red poles—enforcers, in the language of the triads. Neither was armed, but their training in martial arts made each man a living, breathing weapon, adept at killing with his bare hands or with virtually any object he could grasp.

Which did not make Jiang safe, by any means. Colombia was known for chaos and endemic violence that claimed the lives of citizens ranging from gutter trash to presidents. Jiang would most certainly remain on guard throughout his visit there, while following the best course for his family.

And if by chance some unforeseen disaster should befall him, he'd left orders for retaliation on a scale undreamed of even by Colombia's jaded barbarians. If nothing else, Jiang knew that he would be avenged.

His preference, of course, was to survive and cut a deal that made him richer than he was already, while expanding the influence of the 14K beyond its tenuous foothold in Latin America. Jiang harbored imperial dreams and was anxious to sit on his throne.

Hotel Charleston, Bogotá

"SPAGHETTI," BRUNO Manzoni said with a sneer, glowering at the room service menu. "What the hell is that supposed to mean, *spaghetti.*"

"It means what it means," Marsilio Bonino replied from his place at the window overlooking Carrera 13.

"It don't mean nothing," Manzoni insisted. "What *kind* of spaghetti, already? Is it *alla carbonara, alla Bolognese, alla chitarra, alla puttanesca,* or what the hell else? This menu, it don't tell me nothing."

"We're not at home," his consigliere said, stating the obvious. "Back in Palermo, if you asked for tacos, would the cook know what you were talking about?"

"See, this is exactly what I mean," Manzoni said. "With these Colombians, we gotta listen close to ever'thing they say. They'll try and screw us anyway they can."

"We do the same," Bonino said.

"But that's legitimate. It's for the Family."

"That's the truth," Bonino agreed.

"They want to trade cocaine for some heroin, we can deal. The guns, okay. Maybe they can help us hide a few of our brothers while the heat's on, back at home. But everywhere they go, there's trouble. Headlines, we don't need."

"No publicity," Bonino agreed.

The television had been playing with its sound muted, some kind of soap opera where everybody seemed to be shouting and carrying on like a bunch of hysterical idiots. Manzoni was turning away from the set when a newscast cut in with live footage of a building on fire.

"Turn that up," he commanded, and one of his men hopped to it, snagging the remote and raising the volume. Not that it helped, with the voice-over coming in Spanish.

The scene showed cops in uniform looking at bodies in the street, covered with sheets. One of the young reporter's words jumped out at Manzoni: *narcoterroristas.*

"Shit!" he swore. "You hear that?"

"Something about a terrorist," Bonino said.

"Not just any old terrorist," Manzoni corrected his aide. "She mentioned narcotics."

"Ah. You think it has to do with our guy, then?"

"The hell should I know? Half the people in this country either make cocaine or else smuggle it. I don't like seeing this before we have our meeting, though. I'll tell you that for free."

"Planes fly both ways," Bonino said. "You want me to, I'll call the airport immediately and book a flight back home. Forget this whole damn business."

"No," Manzoni said. "My whole damn life, I never ran away from anything." Which was a lie, as they both knew, since he'd been a fugitive from justice in his homeland for the past four years, convicted in absentia of assorted crimes including murder and extortion. Still, it sounded good.

"You want to stay, we stay," Bonino said. "You're the boss."

Which was true. Manzoni *was* the boss—at least, in Sicily. But here in Bogotá, he realized, it would be wise to watch his step.

Since any one he took could be his last.

15

They were back where they'd begun, cruising past the Andino Mall in midmorning traffic, with workmen milling around the sidewalk café where Jack Styles and so many bystanders had died in the blast of Macario's opening shot. Bolan didn't keep score during battle, had no firm idea of how many had died since the bomb's detonation had launched his campaign in Colombia, but he knew more would die before it was done.

Pureza, on her cell with one of her connections from the CNP, was saying, "*Sí...sí... Qué?... Ah, sí... Comprendo... Sí... Mil gracias... Y usted, también... Adios.*"

Closing the phone at last, she said, "All right, I have it."

"Go ahead," he urged.

"The CNP was tracking the arrival of some foreigners. Five men from each of five different countries. The parties are staying at different downtown hotels. I have the names here," she said, lifting a spiral notebook.

"You said the CNP *was* tracking them? Past tense?"

"That's right. An order came to break off all surveillance. It was by—"

"Your deputy vice-minister," Bolan said, guessing.

"Right again. The bastard Guzman."

"Works for me," Bolan replied. "I'd rather not run into any cops if I can help it while we're wrapping up this thing."

"We're going after them?" she asked. Pureza's voice had taken on a worried tone.

"Hard to resist those kinds of targets," Bolan said.

"But five hotels in downtown Bogotá! The traffic and police patrols! Why, we don't even know their room numbers."

"And that's exactly why we'll pass on the hotels," Bolan replied. "Macario won't shuttle back and forth to meet them individually. He wants all of them together. Otherwise, he'd do his business on the phone."

"So they must gather," Pureza said.

"Like sitting ducks," Bolan agreed.

"But where's the pond?" she asked, soft-spoken, as if questioning herself. "Someplace Macario controls."

"Must be. He wouldn't trust security to anybody else with this much riding on the line."

"He has a large estate in Usaquén," she said. "Off Avenida Laureano Gomez, near the country club. The neighborhood is called La Carolina."

"And when you say large, you mean…?"

"Forty or fifty acres, I'm not sure," Pureza replied. "I know there is an eight-foot wall around the property, with only one gate. Under guard, of course. Besides the tennis court, gymnasium and swimming pool, he also has a helicopter landing pad."

"So, two ways in and out," Bolan said.

"And we can't use either one of them," Pureza said.

"Just means we'll have to find a third. Any idea what kind of force he keeps around the place?" Bolan inquired.

"A dozen men on average," she said. "For this kind of fiesta, double that, or maybe triple it. Then servants in the house, mostly unarmed. Women perhaps, for entertainment of his guests."

A crowd, in other words, Bolan thought, with maybe two-thirds of them packing heat and primed to cut down any party crashers they found roaming on the grounds. The guests of honor would arrive by car, most likely, but could flee by air in an emergency.

Or, could they?

"Can you tell me any more about the helipad? What kind of chopper does he use?"

"Macario has two at this place that I know of. One that I've seen is fairly small. It might seat four or five, at most."

"The other one?" he pressed.

"It's larger. Like a military aircraft. I don't know the model."

The description was vague, but it helped. The military UH-1D Iroquois, nicknamed "Huey" in Vietnam and beyond, could carry fourteen passengers besides its crew. The larger CH-47 "Chinook" could seat fifty-five besides crew in a pinch, but it was ninety-nine-feet long, with a sixty-foot rotor diameter—unlikely, in short, to set down in a posh neighborhood without causing one hell of a fuss.

So when the crunch came, if Macario tried getting out by air, he'd likely have a Huey standing by. And with himself aboard, even as crew, it meant that he could only rescue fourteen of his personnel, at most. A UH-1D could carry El Padrino's top ten VIPs to safety, if they left their bodyguards behind.

But they'd have to reckon with the Executioner.

"IT MUST BE PERFECT. No errors, nothing out of place. Do you understand?"

"Yes, sir." Macario's chef and valet nodded in unison, the latter gulping nervously. When El Padrino clamored for perfection, anyone who let him down might literally disappear.

"Go on, then!" he commanded. "Do your jobs and make me proud!"

"Yes, sir."

Santiago Villegas observed the ritual and knew he had to be next. Macario had questioned him intently, as to the security arrangements for their guests, and while the answers seemed to satisfy him, one could never know for sure.

"The limousines have been dispatched?" Macario inquired.

"All gone, sir."

"They must arrive at each hotel precisely at the same time."

"I informed the drivers," Villegas replied, "and made them synchronize their watches."

"Good. We must expect some small delay, loading the passengers. Russians, I'm told, have small regard for time."

"They'll be encouraged, sir. Gently and politely."

"It's the best that we can do, eh, Santiago?"

"You're correct, sir."

"And the arrangements here?"

"Forty soldiers," Villegas replied, hoping that forty would satisfy El Padrino. "Half are hidden, so that your guests do not become alarmed."

"Good thinking," Macario said. His frown deepened as he inquired, "Has there been any word of Esteban?"

"Not yet, sir. We have men at the airport, but he wouldn't be that foolish. Maybe if he drove to Medellín or Cali he could fly. We have surveillance on the highways, also, but he might switch cars."

"I want him *alive*, to answer for his treachery!" Macario snarled.

"The men have been informed, sir. Your offer to the men who capture him is very generous. I've added an incentive by reminding them that anyone who kills him must assume his fate."

"Excellent! I trust they'll remember that, when he is in their gunsights."

"You may count on it, sir."

"It seems you've thought of everything," Macario said.

Villegas shrugged, all modesty. "Under your guidance, I live but to serve."

"I reward loyalty," Macario reminded him. "You know that."

"Yes, sir."

"And I punish treason."

"As you should, sir."

"Perhaps Esteban lost his nerve. Perhaps he was a coward all along and managed to deceive me."

"Doubtful, sir. With your skill at judging character, you would have found him out."

"In any case, he's taught me to examine those I trust. You understand?"

"Yes, sir."

"I'll be watching you. Succeed, and you will prosper. Fail…"
He left the statement hanging, turned away to scold a housekeeper
who wasn't dusting fast enough to suit him.

Villegas, duly warned, had no intention of failing his master.
Sheer luck had granted him a chance to fill Quintaro's shoes—he
had to outshine Macario's old lieutenant in all things.

And if he could deliver Esteban Quintaro to his fate of
wretched agonizing death, so much the better for himself. It
would be the icing on the cake.

PIRRO AZNAR WAS PLOTTING strategy with maps spread before
him when Léon Rivera appeared in the doorway, holding the
satellite phone. Aznar glared at his second in command and
growled, "What?"

"You have another call," Rivera said.

"I sensed that. Who is it?"

"I think," Rivera said, "the one who called before."

He didn't have to say which one. Only two calls had been
received within the past twelve hours, one of them from Naldo
Macario and the other from the nameless man who warned of
El Padrino's treachery.

"I'll take it," Aznar said. He reached out for the phone, feeling
as if a brick had settled in his stomach. Into the phone he said,
"You wish to trouble me again?"

"Or help you out," the caller said. "Depends on how you look
at it."

"What makes you think I need your help?" Aznar inquired
stiffly.

"Your operations have been taking hits all over Bogotá, and
I don't see you hitting back. I'd like to help you change that."

"You are very generous, *señor*." Aznar made no attempt to
hide his sneer.

The caller let it pass and said, "Macario's throwing a party at
his place in La Carolina, out by the golf course. You know it?"

Aznar ignored the question, countered with one of his own.
"What kind of party?"

"For the rich and infamous," the caller said. "He's got all

kinds of people coming in from Asia, Europe and the States to talk about business, nail down alliances, find himself some new partners."

Aznar knew this already, but decided to hear out the caller.

"And I am supposed to believe this because…?"

"Hey, have I ever lied to you? The tip about your newspaper office—"

"*Sí, sí.* About the foreigners you claim are coming—"

"Yakuza, triads, the Mafia, some Russian hoods. All dropping in to have a look at Bogotá. Maybe deciding if they'd like to buy a piece of it and set up shop."

"And you hope that I will…what? Attack these foreigners? Declare a war against Macario?"

"You're late on that one," the caller said. "He's already declared war on you. As for the rest, I'm in the information business, not the planning side. Do what you want. Maybe that's nothing. Sit and wait for Naldo and his new friends to come looking for you in a pack. No skin off me."

Again the link was broken, giving Aznar no chance to reply. Rivera stood waiting at his side.

"Macario's guests have arrived," Aznar told him at last. "A group of foreign criminals. Their plans remain unclear. I wish to make their time in Bogotá a memorable one."

Rivera smiled at that and asked, "Where are they gathering?"

"If we believe this one—" he nodded toward the phone in Rivera's hand "—it will be Naldo's home beside the country club."

"A well-protected meeting place," Rivera said.

"But not invincible."

"No, Pirro."

"There are walls, if I remember rightly."

"Yes."

"So we must be prepared to scale them or to take them down."

"Why not prepare for both?" Rivera asked.

"Why not, indeed. Collect explosives, also ropes. And find some grappling hooks."

"Yes, Pirro."

"Naldo wants to throw a party," Aznar said. "But we can furnish the surprise."

NALDO MACARIO WAS READY when the first of his imported guests arrived at his estate in La Carolina. The place was spotless, all the liquor and hors d'oeuvres were ready, served by beautiful young women chosen for their willingness to offer special services upon demand. Guards were in place, without being obtrusive, with two-thirds of them concealed and killing time upstairs. The house was large enough that individuals—or even groups of men—could disappear and not be missed.

As some had, on occasion, never being seen again.

The Americans, Ciampi and d'Arezzo, were first to arrive. Macario greeted them both with smiles and handshakes, asked about their flight as anyone might do.

"I've been on better planes," Ciampi said. "And that includes the one that took me to Atlanta for a three-year jolt in ninety-one. At least they didn't charge me first-class rates for third-class service."

"Well," Macario replied, struggling to keep his smile in place, "I trust that your hotel accommodations please you and that everything I offer you tonight shall satisfy."

"Tall order, that," Ciampi said. "I'll let you know how it works out."

"Of course. If I may show you to the bar…"

He hoped that alcohol and cleavage might combine to soften the disgruntled capo's mood. If not, Ciampi's attitude might well infect the others, or at least discourage them from joining in an enterprise that might include him.

Next to cross his threshold were the Russians, Anton Gergiev and Tikhon Polekh. Both were lean, with long hair, stubble darkening their jaws and tattoos peeking from the open collars of their shirts. Their handshakes stopped just short of causing pain.

Macario went through his spiel, receiving no complaints this time, and asked how they were finding Bogotá.

"It's smaller than Saint Petersburg, but nice enough," Gergiev said. "I like the women here."

"You may be pleased to meet my staff," Macario suggested.

"The last time that I was in Colombia," Polekh said, "I recall some crazy fuckers tried to kill me in Guajira."

"Crazy fuckers are the rule up there," Macario agreed. "We've tried to weed them out."

"If you need any help with that," Polekh said, "let me know. I'd love to pay them back for nearly shooting off my balls."

"Tikhon values his balls," Gergiev said.

"It's like they're part of me," Polekh replied.

Macario began to feel as if the smile was carved into his face. He led the Russians to the open bar and introduced them to the Yanquis, leaving them to entertain each other while he left to meet the next arriving party.

Chinese, this time, their faces perfect masks concealing all emotion. As he greeted them, Macario allowed his head to dip a little, not quite bowing, since he owed servility to no man living. Handshakes followed as he introduced himself to each in turn, by rank, their faces recognized from photographs.

When it was done, Jiang Kemin said, "You have invited members of the Yakuza as well, we understand?"

"You are correct," Macario replied. "I strive for peace, cooperation and mutual profit."

"Except in Bogotá, apparently," Liu Xian said. "The television broadcasts hourly reports of slaughter and destruction in the streets."

Macario felt heat flare in his cheeks. "A matter soon to be resolved," he said. "You have my word on that."

"Presumably ensured by deeds," Jiang remarked.

"You may be sure of it," Macario replied, and led them off to meet their peers.

Usaquén District, Bogotá

"Do you believe Aznar will take your bait?" Pureza asked Bolan.

"If I had to guess, I'd call it eighty-twenty," he replied. "We won't count on it, but it couldn't hurt."

"It won't take long before the neighbors call the police," she said, "even with El Padrino's walls and spacious grounds. I won't fire at them."

"I won't, either," Bolan said. He caught her look and added, "It's a rule."

"A rule?"

"One of my own. Cops are exempt, even the ones who don't deserve it."

"What about Guzman?" she asked, frowning.

"He's not a cop," Bolan replied. "Guzman's a politician and a parasite. Fair game."

"You have a strange code, Matt."

Bolan shrugged and said, "It works for me."

"But there are officers who rape and murder. Aren't they criminals, as much as Guzman or Macario?"

He nodded. "Sure they are, and I sometimes make an exception. But not often. Once you start down that road, where does it end?"

"Where does your own road end?" she asked him solemnly.

"Same place as everybody else's," Bolan said. "I may get there ahead of them and miss the golden years, but on the brighter side, you'll never find me strapped into a wheelchair at a so-called rest home, trying to remember my own name."

"So, you're a fatalist," she said.

"A *realist*. Some soldiers quit after a while and fade away, like Doug MacArthur said. The ones who stick will go down fighting someday, somewhere. It's a fact of life. No one gets out alive."

"You chose this life," she said.

"Correct."

"But why?"

He had to smile at that. "Seemed like a good idea at the time," he replied. "Still does, in fact."

"You might have had a family."

"I do," he said, thinking of Hal Brognola, Able Team and Phoenix Force, the gang at Stony Man Farm, and those who'd fallen on the long, hard road. "Just not the usual."

"Someone to love?" she asked.

He wasn't going there. "It isn't a romantic life, I grant you. Not a lot of time for dating, picnics or what-have-you."

"But you don't regret your choices."

"No," he answered honestly.

"Or worry that today may be your last day?"

"Worrying's a waste of time and energy," Bolan said. "Make your preparations, do the best you can and face the unexpected when it happens. It's the best that anyone can do. Why add an ulcer to the mix?"

"If you were Japanese, you'd be a samurai," she said.

"I don't look all that great in a kimono. And the hair, forget about it."

"But the spirit, eh? What is it called?"

"Bushido," Bolan said. "The way of the warrior."

"Exactly. That's you."

"Don't start to look for shining armor," Bolan said. "There isn't any."

"But there *is*," Pureza insisted. "When you fought to save the children—"

Bolan cut her off, saying, "We need to focus on what happens next. Has there been any kind of aerial surveillance on Macario's estate?"

"Not that I'm aware of. If there was, I haven't seen the photos."

"Never mind. There's someone I can call," he said, thinking of Brognola. He had no clear idea of how long it would take, or if there might be satellite photos on file at Stony Man Farm, maybe retrievable from sources at the DEA or CIA. In any case, it would be worth a try.

"And when you have them?" Pureza asked.

"If I can get them soon enough, we'll know the layout. Where and how to make the best approach."

"But if they're not available..."

"We go in blind," Bolan replied.

It wouldn't be the first time.

And with any luck, it wouldn't prove to be the last.

16

"My friends, welcome to this, the first of what I hope may be many productive meetings between us for mutual prosperity."

Macario raised his champagne glass, beaming self-confidence and wishful thinking toward the members of his solemn audience. So far, not one of them had cracked a smile since they'd arrived.

"I wish to thank our guests for answering my invitation and for traveling so far from home—Japan, Hong Kong, the Russian Federation, Sicily and from New York. I trust our conversations in the next two days will forge alliances where none currently exist, and help solidify cooperation where it has been practiced."

Ten pairs of eyes examined El Padrino as if he were a performer on a stage, touting his skill at magic, building up to some illusion which might either dazzle them or leave them gravely disappointed. And with *these* men, disappointment often landed someone in a grave.

Macario did not fear them individually, but the groups they led and represented held enormous power worldwide. Conflict with one could damage his cartel. Hostilities engaged with all of them at once would be disastrous. The loss in cocaine revenue alone might bankrupt him, and falling profits always made subordinates consider switching chiefs.

"To friendship and cooperation!" he declared, and drained

his glass. Around him, shifting glances clearly showed that his important guests were not convinced, but all of them were courteous enough to sip their chilled champagne.

Macario knew some of those whom he'd invited already had working relationships. America's Cosa Nostra and the Sicilian Mafia were two sides of a coin; one had sprung from the other, and they remained in profitable contact despite countless fratricidal conflicts among their several Families.

As for the rest…

The Russians were relative upstarts, rising to prominence only since the collapse of Soviet communism in 1991, while the other criminal societies were centuries old. In theory, the Russians dealt with anyone who could put money in their pockets, but they also acted impulsively, rode roughshod over established territories, and sometimes turned friends into sworn enemies.

With the triads and the Yakuza, centuries of national and ethnic rivalry stood in the way of any meaningful collaboration. Macario was no academic historian, but he knew that China and Japan had fought several full-scale wars over the past hundred-plus years, from the nineteenth century through World War II. Millions had died in those conflicts, while the seeds of racial hatred fell on fertile, blood-drenched soil. In crime, competition for opium grown and refined in Asia's Golden Triangle sparked continuing battles in Laos, Myanmar, Thailand and Vietnam.

In short, he faced a Herculean task. But if he could—

The crack of an explosion somewhere on the grounds made El Padrino wince. His guests began to mutter, and he heard one of the Chinese ask another, "Fireworks?"

Jesus Christ! Macario thought. Not here! Not now!

THE FARM HAD COME THROUGH with a satellite photo depicting the layout of Macario's estate. It was a dated snapshot, nothing current being possible on such short notice, but it suited Bolan's needs. He'd seen the mansion with its helipad, tennis courts and Olympic-size swimming pool, its servants quarters and six-car garage set on manicured and lightly wooded grounds. It was an urban refuge for the rich and shameless, all surrounded by the eight-foot wall Pureza had described.

They needed a diversion while they scaled that barrier, so Bolan put his MM-1 to work. One high-explosive round lofted across the wall, aimed vaguely toward the northeast corner of the property where nothing had been built. He'd used an airburst round, to rule out any possibility that soft earth might defeat his purpose, and was ready when the blast echoed through darkness.

First, he gave Pureza a boost and saw her disappear over the wall. Next Bolan leaped, caught hold with practiced hands and hauled himself aloft. He spent a fraction of a moment on the wall, adjusting weapons for the drop, then plummeted to join Pureza on the ground.

They were inside, step one, but far from anything resembling victory. Bolan unslung his M-4 carbine, left the 40 mm launcher strapped across his back for the moment and led the way toward El Padrino's lavish mansion. Pureza ran beside him, carrying the silenced Spectre SMG, with the Benelli shotgun slung.

Somewhere in the palace, the chiefs of state for syndicated crime worldwide were gathered to receive Macarlo's proposal for a new alliance. If Bolan could eliminate them it would send shock waves around the world, from Manhattan to Hong Kong to Saint Petersburg.

So many targets and so little time.

The first explosion might have triggered phone calls to police, but Bolan hoped it would be passed off as an inexplicable anomaly, confusing neighbors without triggering hysterical alarm. That hope would vanish once the shooting started, though, and that could happen anytime.

Like now.

A sentry who had lagged behind while others ran off to investigate the fireworks loomed out of the night, snapping at them in Spanish, leveling an automatic weapon. Bolan shot him in the chest without a heartbeat's hesitation, saw him fall and knew the feces was about to hit the fan.

"Come on!" he told Pureza, and broke into a sprint toward El Padrino's home.

MORI SABURO HEARD THE stutter of automatic gunfire in the night and instantly stepped closer to his aide and bodyguards. Naldo Macario approached them, trying to maintain his smile but failing.

"It is likely nothing," the Colombian assured his guests, convincing none among them with his tone or his expression.

"Are your guards so poorly trained they shoot at nothing?" Mori asked.

"I can assure you—"

More gunfire, spreading and moving closer to the house. Macario dropped the facade and made off toward the kitchen with its exit on the south side of the mansion.

A babble of excited voices rose in the reception room. One of the suet-faced Sicilians called for guns. A tattooed Russian shouted that they had been lured into a trap. One of the richly groomed Americans said, "Fuck this shit! I'm outta here!"

But where could any of them go?

Mori did not believe Macario planned to eliminate them. If he did, why were his soldiers firing in the yard, instead of in the room where all his guests were assembled? Still, based on what Mori had seen on television in his hotel room, the meeting *could* be a trap of sorts, staged by Macario's enemies.

One thing was clear—the sooner Mori's party could depart from Macario's home, the better off they would be. But how?

Mori supposed one of his men could drive the limousine that had delivered them—if they could find the keys, avoid Macario's armed guards and somehow breach the gates—then find their slow way back to the Lugano Imperial Suites, pack their bags and catch the next flight out of Bogotá. But with a firefight clearly underway, those relatively simple acts became more difficult. Perhaps impossible.

Mori turned to his guards. "Find weapons," he instructed.

"Any sort that you can use. We must be ready to defend ourselves and seek a way out of this place."

"You will be safe here, Mori-san?" one of the soldiers asked.

"If you're not gone too long," Mori replied. "Be swift in your return to us."

"Hai!" the guards said in unison before they left in opposite directions, seeking anything at hand within the banquet room that might be used for self-defense.

Mori himself spotted a chef's knife on the serving line, lying beside a roast of beast. It was the kind of knife masked killers often used in horror films, with a wedge-shaped blade at least twelve inches long and razor-sharp along one edge. Feeling a little better when the knife was in his hand and held point-downward at his side, Mori returned to Kanata Hitoshi, who clutched a wine bottle to serve as a bludgeon.

"Be ready when the moment comes for us to flee," he told his second in command. "We may have but a single chance."

STEALTH WAS UNNECESSARY now, but Pureza still wielded her silenced submachine gun, holding the Benelli shotgun in reserve. A moment after Bolan shot the first guard they had met, two more came toward them from the house, firing short bursts from automatic rifles on the run.

Pureza felt a bullet pluck her left sleeve as she threw herself aside and tumbled through an awkward shoulder roll, the shotgun bruising her, eliciting a grunt of pain. She kept her focus, even so, and came up firing with the SMG, stitching the nearer of the gunmen with a 4-round burst across his chest.

By then, Bolan had dropped the other man and was advancing toward the manor house. Pureza scrambled to her feet once more and followed him, sparing a backward glance in the direction they had come from, toward the corner where his air-burst round had detonated. She saw flashlight beams probing the night there, seeking nonexistent enemies, but even in the heartbeat she spent watching them, a couple of the lights were turned in her direction, toward the sounds of gunfire.

No more time to waste.

"They're after us, Matt," she warned Bolan.

"They would be," he replied without a break in stride.

Still not a worrier, even if they were surrounded by their enemies on hostile turf, badly outnumbered, with the prospects for survival looking perilously slim. At least she wouldn't have to suffer through old age with all its pains, Pureza thought, and nearly laughed aloud.

But if she started laughing, Pureza knew that it would quickly lapse into hysterics, ending only when a bullet claimed her life. There might be time for acting crazy soon enough, but for the moment she had to focus on the brutal task at hand.

Another soldier came at them, backlit by the mansion's flood-lights that reduced him to a silhouette. Pureza and Bolan fired as one, impossible to say whose bullet killed the faceless gunman, and it hardly mattered once the job was done.

When she was dead, her parents would be told she'd been a murderer. That label—true enough, under the letter of the law— would stain her family forever, blight her sister and the niece or nephew Pureza would never see. For the first time in at least a dozen years, she thought about the prospect of an afterlife, wondered if there was anything beyond this mortal plane.

And instantly decided that it didn't matter.

She had picked her course—it was too late to change it. All she could do was fight.

And try to stay alive.

"THAT IS THE HOUSE," Léon Rivera said, pointing. "I'm sure of it."

Riding with windows down, Pirro Aznar could hear the pop and rattle of gunfire that echoed through the night, apparently originating from the grounds of El Padrino's walled estate.

"What's happening?" he asked of no one in particular.

"A celebration?" his driver suggested.

"Sounds more like a war," another of Aznar's soldiers said.

"Still a party for us," Aznar said, grinning fiercely.

He had packed twenty-five men into four SUVs, a tight fit

with their weapons, but still possible. More troops had been summoned from outlying districts, but Aznar had feared waiting for
them and missing his chance to attack while Macario's foreign
associates enjoyed his hospitality.

It seemed that someone else had had the same idea.

"Are we going ahead?" his driver asked, confused.

"Absolutely!" Aznar answered. "Hurry!"

The driver hurried, as ordered, but didn't look happy about
it. Approaching the gate they saw one man on guard behind
heavy wrought iron. He turned to face them, framed in Aznar's
headlights, clutching an Uzi SMG.

The guard seemed slightly dazed, so Aznar took a chance.
Leaned from his open window, calling out, "We're here to
help!"

"Who sent you?" the lookout demanded.

"El Padrino called us," Aznar said, ducking the question as
he opened his door and stepped out of the car.

"What is your name?"

Instead of giving his name on demand, Aznar raised his
FMK-3 submachine gun and fired through the bars of the gate,
striking the watchman with three or four rounds out of six. One
bullet struck the gate and whined off into darkness.

"Fabian," Aznar called to one of the backseat soldiers. "Get
over the wall and open the gate. Gabriel, help him up!"

It was an awkward scramble, but Fabian cleared the wall after
forty agonizing seconds, huffing as he came back to the gate,
found its controls and set the wrought-iron barrier rattling open
along buried tracks. Aznar was back in the SUV's shotgun seat
well before the vehicle surged forward, stopped again to retrieve
its two passengers, then rolled ahead toward Macario's home.

"WE'RE GETTING OUT OF here," Anton Gergiev said.

"How, then?" Tikhon Polekh inquired.

"Pick up some guns," Gergiev said. "Do anything we must to
get away."

"I think they don't give up their guns so easy," Aleksey Velten,
one of Gergiev's soldiers, said.

"I don't care what's easy," Gergiev replied. "We get them anyway."

"There go more men," their other soldier, Yuri Ekster, said. He nodded toward a passageway beyond the large reception room, where men with automatic weapons passed an open doorway walking two and three abreast.

"And here we go," Gergiev said, immediately moving off in that direction. No one followed them, the other four-man groups huddling together, speaking urgently as they reacted to the sounds of battle from outside.

Gergiev reached the doorway just as the last two riflemen passed. He called out to them, beckoning when they delayed, then finally approached him, frowning.

"Can you tell us what is happening?" he asked.

"We don't know yet," one of the pair replied.

"Well, then, can you explain—"

And with a snarl, Gergiev smashed his elbow into the closer gunman's face, feeling his nose crack and flatten on impact. Polekh swung at him, too, driving a fist into the young man's gut and emptying his lungs, while Ekster and Velten grabbed the other one and rode him down, wrenching the rifle from his hands and slamming it into his face.

"Check for pistols," Gergiev ordered, once the stragglers lay still and he held one of their automatic weapons. Each unmoving body yielded a handgun and spare magazines. Gergiev recognized his rifle as a Heckler & Koch G3A4 with a collapsible stock and a 20-round magazine.

"What next?" Polekh asked, as he cradled a Galil assault rifle with side-folding stock.

"We get out of here," Gergiev said. "By any means required. Our meeting with Macario is finished."

Gergiev led his small party back in the direction that Macario's soldiers had come from, meeting no more on the way. They passed a staircase leading upward, then an entrance to a large kitchen where staff in white shirts and aprons stirred pots and moved skillets from stovetops to counters.

Their dinner was going to waste, and Gergiev couldn't care less.

He sought an exit from the mansion, access to the limousines or any other vehicle that might transport them from Macario's estate to somewhere safer. He had no interest in remaining where they were, facing interrogation by Colombian police even if El Padrino's soldiers won the fight raging outside.

No interest, certainly, in being held for trial on any charge the local prosecutors might concoct to please themselves, the DEA or anybody else. Escape was paramount, and Gergiev knew he could trust only himself to manage it correctly.

FIFTY YARDS FROM THE mansion and closing, Bolan saw gunmen begin spilling out through a door at the rear. Behind him, at the same time, he could hear the others he'd distracted for a moment with his air-burst HE round returning to the fight.

Instead of counting enemies as they emerged from Macario's mansion, Bolan sprayed them with 5.56 mm tumblers from his M-4 carbine, emptying its magazine on autofire. Beside him, Pureza was blazing away with her Spectre, its muffled stutter drowned by other sounds of combat, but the impact of its bullets visible downrange, where human targets lurched, jerked, spun and fell.

Startled survivors beat a swift retreat into the mansion, their parting shots hasty and wasted. Pureza chased them with the last shots from her first 50-round mag, then bent to reload while Bolan turned to face the yard men rushing at them from behind.

He tugged the MM-1 free of its shoulder sling, hefted its weight and started firing from the hip. The trigger-pull was stiff but manageable, the *pong* sound of the big weapon's muted reports almost comical.

But there was nothing humorous about the impact of those rounds on Bolan's enemies. He'd loaded the fat cylinder with a mix of high explosive and buckshot canister rounds, one HE already gone when he turned to meet Macario's charging minions.

A 40 mm buckshot round contained twenty-seven double-00

pellets, each equivalent to a .33-caliber bullet. A single shot aimed waist-high cut through the hostile ranks like a scythe, leaving bloody ruin in its wake, while the HE follow-up sent bodies tumbling through the air. Screams and wailing rose as another charge dissolved in blood.

Bolan used the momentary respite to reload his carbine, ditching its spent magazine and slapping a new one into place. He scanned the yard for stragglers, then turned back toward the house, advancing once more with Pureza beside him.

Someone smashed the glass out of a window on the mansion's west wall, on the second floor, and started firing at them from above. They both returned fire, ducking as they did, and someone tagged the sniper, sent his weapon spinning from the window to the shrubbery below.

No sooner was that done than Bolan heard a shout raised from the southwest corner of the mansion, toward its broad veranda. More soldiers emerged from the front door there, circling back to join the fight. Cursing and firing from the hip, they came to meet the Executioner.

17

Santiago Villegas bellowed at his soldiers, driving them out of the house in a rush to meet the unseen enemy. "Out there! Now! Go!"

But how could they kill someone who seemed more and less than human, capable of a strike here and there, then disappearing like a shadow when the lights came on? The gunfire and explosions audible from El Padrino's grounds told him the battle was not going well for the defenders.

Villegas stood in the doorway, prepared to follow his men, but a rush of headlights along the curving driveway managed to distract him. He could see the wrought-iron gate was open and apparently unguarded. Who was this arriving at the worst possible moment? And where had they come from?

His first question was answered seconds later, when he recognized the grinning face of Pirro Aznar, leader of the AUC, protruding from an open window of the lead vehicle. Shouting curses, Aznar thrust a submachine gun from his window and triggered a burst toward the house, stitching a line of bullet holes across its formerly pristine facade.

Villegas dropped to the stone patio, crawling lizardlike for the cover of a nearby ornate brick-and-mortar railing. It would shelter him from pistol rounds fired from an SMG, but slugs from any high-powered assault rifles would penetrate and find him if he didn't find some more substantial cover soon.

Clutching his own weapon, an Argentinean FARA 83 assault rifle with folding stock, Villegas wormed his way across the broad veranda, looking for a point from which he could return incoming fire without exposing too much of himself. He found it in the space between two upright pillars of the railing, just as Aznar's SUV slid to a stop in front of the mansion, three more braking close behind it.

Villegas was ready when doors started popping open on the attacking vehicles, squeezing off short bursts of 5.56 mm NATO rounds at a range of less than twenty feet. Aznar's driver was the first to fall, drilled through the upper chest and throat. Swinging sharply to his left, Villegas framed Aznar himself in the FARA's tritium sights, then saw his target dropping as he fired, hit through the shoulder but alive—for the time being.

Despite the fables spun by Hollywood, where heroes suffered shoulder wounds and still fought on as if unscathed, a real-life hit to that vicinity was crippling, often lethal. The clavicle lay there, together a crucial ball-and-socket joint, various large muscles and the thoracoacromial artery. Villegas didn't know the medical lingo, but he'd seen men bleed to death from shoulder wounds and hoped that Aznar would soon join their number.

Meanwhile, he was taking more fire from the other invaders, pinned down and fighting for his life.

"Did anybody see the fuckin' Russians split?"

Fausto Ciampi's question seemed to startle the remaining guests still gathered in Macario's reception room while chaos reigned outside the mansion. Fifteen other pairs of eyes began to rake the room, seeking Saint Petersburg's contingent without finding them.

"It seems they have departed," one of the Chinese replied. It killed Ciampi how they always talked so formally, regardless of the circumstances.

"Not a bad idea, I'd say," Ciampi told the others. "This joint is goin' to hell in a hurry. Last one out's a fuckin' stiff."

"An' where we go?" one of the old Sicilians challenged him. "You gonna run out *there* and take your chances empty-handed, eh?"

"At least we'd have a chance," d'Arezzo answered, as loyal as ever. "Stay in here, we're just a buncha sitting ducks."

"We need gun," one of the Yakuza members suggested.

"No shit," Ciampi said. "There's gotta be some around here. Fuckin' dealers are always armed to the eyeballs."

"We coulda asked Macario," d'Arezzo said, "if he hadn't run off like a goddamn coward."

And the man he'd called a coward chose that moment to return. "Please, gentlemen, be calm!" their host suggested. "I have planned for everything."

Ciampi felt the angry color rising in his face. "You mean to say you *knew* this shit was comin' down tonight?"

"Of course not," Macario said. "But I've arranged security for any possible event."

"From what I hear outside, the plan ain't workin'," Ciampi replied.

"My men will hold the intruders at bay," Macario assured them, sounding confident. "While we evacuate by air."

"You got a plane in the garage?" d'Arezzo asked.

"A helicopter standing by," Macario corrected him. "You would not see it coming from the street."

Ciampi hated helicopters with their bubble noses, their vibrations and hellacious noise—but what other choice was there? He hadn't flown twenty-five hundred miles from home to stand around and let himself get wasted in some asshole dealer's private war.

Screw that.

"Awright," Ciampi said. "You got a bird with seats enough for all of us, let's see it. The sooner we get the hell outta this madhouse, the better I'll like it."

"Us, too," the oldest of the four Sicilians said. The Chinese and the Japanese just nodded, while they looked askance at one another, frowning.

"Very well," their host said, turning toward the nearest exit from the banquet room. "Then follow me."

BOLAN COULDN'T SAY EXACTLY how he had been separated from Pureza. One moment they were entering the house, stepping around the body of a lone defender who had tried to block their entry, covering a spacious pantry-type room with two exits. The next, incoming fire was ripping at them from behind, outside the house, and they were scrambling for cover while watching the doors for new threats.

Bolan met one almost instantly. A lanky gunner with shoulder-length hair barged through the nearest doorway, advancing behind a Kalashnikov rifle and looking for targets. Before he could find one, a round from outside struck his left arm and spun him off balance, leaving Bolan to finish the kill with a short burst from his M-4.

He'd turned then, looking for Pureza, and found himself alone. Knowing she hadn't run outside into the storm of hostile fire, he reckoned that she had to have used the other exit from the pantry. Going where, exactly? Bolan couldn't say and didn't have the time to launch a search.

Cursing, he forged ahead, bypassed the freshest corpse and stepped into a hallway evidently leading toward the kitchen and a formal dining room. He'd covered only ten or fifteen yards when four men came around a corner, well downrange, and spotted him. They weren't Latinos—far too pale, for starters—and when one of them called out to Bolan, "Who the fuck are you?" he caught a hint of Eastern Europe in the voice.

Or maybe Russia?

Two of them were packing automatic weapons, while the other two held pistols. Without giving Bolan time to answer their inquiry, all of them cut loose at once, slugs chewing up the walls and ceiling as they got acquainted with their weapons in the first few seconds. Bolan hit the deck, rolled to his left and started firing for effect with his M-4.

It should've been a turkey shoot, but turkeys didn't shoot back. The Russians obviously knew what they were doing. Bolan's slim advantage was his quick reaction time, drilled into him from boot camp onward, turned to second nature by the countless times his own survival had depended on it.

He took the automatic gunners first because their weapons were more dangerous. Rolling across the carpet littered with plaster dust, he stitched them high and low with 5.56 mm manglers, unconcerned with surgical precision, just as long as he scored killing wounds. The shooters fell together, one of them still firing as he crumpled through a sloppy pirouette and sprayed one of his backup gunmen with a final burst from his Kalashnikov.

And that left one.

The lone survivor, to his credit, never gave a thought to running. Rather, he advanced on Bolan, snarling incoherently and rapid-firing with his handgun. Bolan heard a bullet sizzle past his face and felt another draw a line of fire across one calf—a painful graze, but nothing that would slow him appreciably.

And when the Russian fired his last shot, when the slide locked open on his autoloader, Bolan shot him from the floor, a 4-round burst of tumblers shearing off most of his face. The dead man standing toppled over backward, slowly, and went down.

Leaving the Executioner alone, with work to do.

AZNAR BELIEVED THAT HE was dying. He could feel a clammy coldness seeping through his body, robbing him of strength and sapping his will to fight. Before that happened, though, he was determined to remind his enemies that they were dealing with a man, and not someone who sat down and wept when it hurt.

"Help me up!" he demanded, half turning to Rivera. "Come on, help—"

But Rivera was far beyond helping Aznar, or himself for that matter. A bullet had punched through his forehead above the left eye and blown out the back of his skull, spilling Rivera's final thoughts onto the bloody pavement.

"Never mind. You rest there," Aznar told his trusted aide. Setting down his FMK-3 submachine gun, he used his one good hand to clutch the SUV's nearest tire and haul himself from a seated position up to his knees. That effort reawakened the blinding agony in Aznar's mutilated shoulder, but pain was welcome if it cleared the mist out of his brain.

When he had one foot underneath him, Aznar reached down and retrieved his weapon, checking it as best he could one-handed. Thankfully, the FMK-3 was an Uzi clone—a true machine pistol—and Aznar had replaced its spent 40-round magazine before he stepped out of his car and was wounded. If he could just stand, then Macario's men would recognize the kind of soldier who confronted them.

It seemed to take forever, pushing off with one foot, slumped against the SUV for leverage and straining painfully, but Aznar finally succeeded in standing erect. Before he could lose that momentum, he pushed off and lurched toward Macario's porch and front door, raising his submachine gun as if in salute to the gunners whose weapons were blazing away at him from the doorway and windows.

Aznar fired, holding down his SMG's trigger, emptying its magazine in a blaze of fury, less than four seconds' worth, flaying the mansion's facade. And by the time his last bright cartridge casing hit the driveway, he was falling, weighted by the bullets ripping into him, bearing him down into a realm of endless night.

PUREZA HAD NO IDEA WHERE Bolan was, or how to find him. Wandering the halls and calling out his name would be a suicidal act, and likely fruitless. She had lost him by some hasty action of her own, presumably, and was presently on her own.

She had emptied and reloaded her Spectre SMG, then switched it for the shotgun as she prowled the corridors of Macario's mansion. So far, she'd met only two men, blasting both of them dead in their tracks with buckshot. Despite the clamor of battle within and outside, the mansion seemed strangely deserted as she passed through empty rooms and hallways.

Seeking what? The big American? Macario? His foreign visitors? An exit from the house of death? Whatever she was looking for, or what might lie ahead of her, Pureza felt compelled to keep on moving. Standing still, she thought, might cost her life.

Pureza checked her watch and wondered what was keeping the police. It seemed impossible that none of El Padrino's neighbors had called for help yet—preposterous, in fact. Had there been some delay at CNP headquarters? Were they waiting for a unit of the Special Operations Command to assemble and arm itself? Or had someone at headquarters consciously delayed the response?

Someone like Deputy Vice-Minister Cristiano Guzman, perhaps?

Would it serve Guzman's purpose to let Macario sink or swim on his own, while standing back and waiting to mop up the stragglers? If Macario's foreign guests should escape, there'd be no questions asked about their business in Bogotá, and no need for Guzman to explain how his investigators had missed their arrival. If Macario died, it would crimp Guzman's lifestyle, but he also might find new freedom if liberated from El Padrino's grasp.

Something to think about, but at another time, when Pureza wasn't fighting for her life. She ducked into a storage room of some kind, cleared it and spent a moment pondering her options without fear of being shot in the back.

If Macario was wise, he would be fleeing, taking his VIPs with him. The AUC's strike team, glimpsed briefly on arrival as she made her way into the house with Bolan, might have blocked escape by car.

Which left the helipad. And her partner in all this would be heading there, as well, unless she missed her guess.

Scanning the corridor as she emerged, Pureza turned back to retrace her steps and find the pantry where she'd entered El Padrino's home, suddenly worried that she might have missed the main event.

"This way! Hurry!"

The others hardly needed Macario's urging to hurry. They were running, each to the best of his ability, across the sweeping lawn that had become a battlefield. Ahead of them, still fifty yards away, the helicopter squatted on its pad, rotors beginning their slow windup as the pilot ran his checklist, fired the engines and prepared to lift off.

The Huey helicopter could accommodate a four-man crew plus fourteen passengers. Macario had lost his Russians somewhere and was not about to search for them, which left himself, the lone pilot and sixteen foreign guests to fill the freedom bird and make their getaway. If only he could get them all aboard before some bastard came along to stop them.

"Hurry up!" He hastened them along, helping his visitors into the aircraft while three of his soldiers hung back, guarding their flanks. "Move to the rear. Take any seat and buckle in, quickly!"

When all were in their seats and grappling with their safety belts, Macario's men started forward as if to join the rest on board. He blocked them with his body, one foot on the metal steps, hand on the pistol at his belt in case they challenged him and ordered them back to the house.

"Your comrades need you," he reminded them. "Protect the organization. Destroy our enemies, and you will be rewarded."

If you live, he thought, and watched them turn away, downcast, as he boarded the helicopter. They would do as they were told, and die in his defense if need be, like the guard dogs that they were.

"Where are the Russians?" someone asked Macario, as he prepared to close the helicopter's door behind himself.

"They left without us," he replied, neither knowing nor caring if that was the truth.

"Good thing," said one of the Americans. "We got no fuckin' room in here for anybody else."

Macario moved forward, settling into the copilot's seat and fastened the safety belt across his lap. In front of him, he saw a plume of smoke just rising from his mansion and could almost taste it, choking on the bitter flavor of defeat.

But I'm not beaten yet, he thought. Before it's done, I'll hunt you sons of bitches down and kill you all.

BOLAN EMERGED FROM THE mansion and turned toward the helipad in back, already hearing the slow whup-whup-whup of the rotor blades turning, accelerating toward liftoff. He couldn't tell who was aboard, but simple logic told him that the chopper wouldn't fly without Macario aboard. As for his foreign visitors, it stood to reason that he'd try to carry them away, as well.

And if not, they could take care of themselves.

Crossing the broad lawn at a run, he slung his carbine and unlimbered the heavy MM-1. He had nine 40 mm rounds left in the cylinder, with buckshot up next, followed in rotation by HE, an incendiary cartridge, then more buckshot, and so on around the fat drum.

The Huey was rising, already ten feet off the ground and climbing, some eight thousand pounds if its seats were all filled. Bolan recalled the sensation of liftoff, the great beast swaying from side to side in midair as its rotors bit at the air and lifted it skyward.

He could see the pilot's startled face, and Macario beside him in the backup seat, pointing and shouting. There was nothing the pilot could do to halt Bolan's advance, and the ship had no gunners aboard as he closed within striking range, aiming his launcher for point-blank assault.

He squeezed the double-action trigger three times, blasting out the copter's windshield with buckshot that riddled the pilot and left him draped slack in his harness, then followed with HE and chemical fire. Macario was screaming as the Huey dropped to the ground nose-down from an altitude of thirty-odd feet and exploded, first shattered from within, and then consumed by oily leaping flames. A moment later its fuel tanks went up in a double-thump secondary explosion, the shock wave and heat driving Bolan back from the crumpled funeral pyre.

Sudden shotgun blasts behind him made Bolan turn, crouching, in time to see the last of three gunmen collapse on the lawn. Pureza moved past them, lowering her Benelli as she approached.

"Macario?" she asked, with a nod toward the chopper.

"And friends," Bolan said.

"So, we're done here?"

"I'd say so," he answered, as sirens wailed into the night, still far off but approaching at speed.

"Time to go, then," she urged.

Bolan nodded and told her, "I'm already gone."

Epilogue

Cristiano Guzman left his office at 10:47 a.m. on the day after Naldo Macario's fiery demise. He had passed a long, sleepless night at headquarters and spent a grim morning answering questions from his superiors, including the Minister of National Defense himself. It had been touch-and-go, as the Americans might say, explaining why his two Special Operations Commando teams had been late in arriving at Macario's estate, but in the end everyone seemed satisfied with the result.

In fact, Guzman had emerged as something of a hero.

In one swoop, Bogotá had been purged of El Padrino and his top lieutenants, plus Pirro Aznar and a dangerous strike force from the Autodefensas Unidas de Colombia. And if that were not enough to place Guzman's star on the rise, the autopsies were expected to identify the bodies of notorious felons from five foreign countries. A few selective tips to friendly journalists would surely paint him as the man who crushed a global conspiracy of organized crime, all without losing a single innocent bystander.

It was a day for celebration, but first he needed sleep. When he was rested, Guzman would begin working the telephone, stroking his television contacts, perhaps even considering a full-scale press conference. It would be an audacious move, but probably safe if he moved while excitement was high and he was the man of the hour.

As he left the Palace of Justice, walking toward the limousine that waited for him at the curb, Guzman was thinking of the future. More specifically, *his* future. Colombian voters loved heroes, particularly in the present day and age when men of courage and vision were in short supply. Who better to seek higher office in the next election than the man who cleaned up Bogotá?

How high could he aim? The presidency was beyond his grasp, at least for the moment, but some ambitious candidate with solid party backing might appreciate a hero as a running mate. The office of vice president would be a handy launching pad to greater things—or, failing that, why not a seat in Congress?

He reached the limousine, ignored the bodyguard in uniform who held his door open, then closed it after him. The guard took his seat in front, beside the driver, facing forward.

"Mi casa," Guzman said, assuming any driver assigned to the Palace of Justice had to know where he lived.

"Sí, señor," the driver said, startling Guzman with her feminine voice.

A woman chauffeur? He wasn't sure whether to be pleased or insulted, but he clearly could not flirt with her in the bodyguard's presence. Best to ignore her, then, and begin to relax on the ride.

Five minutes later, Guzman saw his turnoff pass and then recede. "You've missed it!" he called out to the driver.

"There has been a change of plans," she replied.

He frowned. "What do you mean, a change of plans?"

The bodyguard half turned in his seat then, revealing a gringo's tanned face and the gun in his hand.

"Relax," Bolan told the would-be hero. "We're just tying up loose ends."